INFERNO 2033

BOOK TWO:

PERDITION

BY

MICHAEL COMPTON
AND
SHERRY J. COMPTON

ORIGINAL STORY
BY
ALLAN J. WALSH

THE JOURNEY PRESS

BOOK TWO

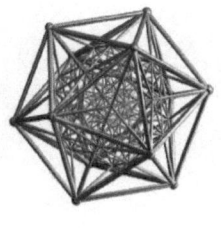

PERDITION

PROLOGUE

Guitars clash like sirens. A tattered American flag ripples, transparent, over scenes of turmoil: Riots in the streets. Confrontations at the border. Trains derailed. Bridges collapsed. Buildings toppled.

A Christmas tree burns like a bonfire.

A pair of evil eyes, like vultures in the billowing smoke, gaze down upon the scene with delight.

Drums come up, and the guitars settle into a pounding rhythm. Jet fighters roar through a blood red sky. Bombs burst. Soldiers march. Guns blaze. The tattered flag catches fire.

But as it burns, instead of turning to ash it is renewed. The transparent rags become solid. The soiled, faded colors become brilliant against a pristine sky.

Rising up, the war-chiseled figure of President William Stockdale looms like a monument, resplendent in his full general's regalia, his elbow cocked, his hand brandished over his brow in a perfect military salute.

At his shoulder, Vice President Henry Brzinski is a watchful shadow in black leather jacket and beret, congruent with the Commander-in-Chief in every form and angle.

As the two men hold their salute, the President's voice rises above the still-driving music:

"When America called, I answered! When America asked, I gave! When America needed a champion, I fought! I bled for you, America! And when I bleed, I bleed red, white, and blue!"

Dissolve to the Stockdale inauguration. As his words resound, the hundreds of thousands gathered on the Mall before the Washington Monument cheer wildly.

An announcer, in voice-of-God cadences, narrates the scene:

"When the citizens of the United States of America elected General William Stockdale as their president, he made three promises...

"Lock out the foreigners!"

Images from the border: A forty-foot, concrete wall. Gun turrets. Militarized checkpoints. Illegals rounded up. Clamoring hordes locked out. A smiling Mr. and Mrs. America, papers in hand, waved through.

"That promise has been kept, with secure borders and ten million illegal aliens expelled."

"Lock up the criminals!"

Images from the streets: A SWAT team swarms a crack house. Terrorists arrested. Flag-burners beaten down. Floating prisons built off-shore. Prisoners frog-marched into waiting cells.

"That promise has been kept, with the Prisoners at Sea Secured program--one hundred new floating prisons built and over five million criminals locked away, far from our shores."

"Free the Citizens!"

Images from heartland America: Combines harvesting wheat. Cowboys driving cattle. Steel workers building skyscrapers. Kids playing baseball. Families going to church. Children running with sparklers. Fireworks.

Flags. Couples ice-skating. A restored Rockefeller Center, with the President playing Santa Claus before its towering Christmas tree.

"That promise has been kept. Our cities have been rebuilt. Our jobs are back. Our streets are safe. And America is standing tall."

The saluting duo emerge again, looming like titans before a rippling flag.

Right on cue, they complete their salute as the announcer declares:

"Promises made. Promises kept!"

The music comes up again. The two figures are marching now, Stockdale holding his bible and revolver like talismans. A phalanx of Americans from every branch of service and walk of life follow in lockstep, marching up Pennsylvania Avenue in time to the rhythm of the music.

A soaring voice sings:

"When they come, will you answer the call?
"When they ask, will you give them your all?
"When they hand you a gun, will you shoot?
"When you bleed, is it red, white, and blue?"

-1-

In spite of the cost of living, it's still popular.
—Kathleen Norris

The song's refrain repeated and faded until the cell monitors throughout the prison ship *Inferno* went silent. It was a catchy tune, and the fact that it was pure propaganda for the government that had built this hellhole didn't keep a few knuckleheads from belting it out like drunks at a party singing karaoke.

Sands knew the song well. Everyone called it "Red, White, and Blue," but the actual title was "Bleed." That was the first clue it was not what it seemed. The song had been a big hit back in the 'twenties—the only hit, as far as Sands knew, by a band called The New Tomfools. No idea what happened to the Old Tomfools, if they ever existed. That was the second clue. The song had been hugely popular among military people, Sands included. But some of the verses had always seemed off to him, and he began to get the idea "Bleed" might not have been the patriotic anthem everyone was so convinced it was.

When he proposed to guys in his unit that the song might actually be *anti*-military, they all looked at him like he was crazy. Irony was a concept that didn't play well in Special Forces. When Sands tried to explain that no one *literally* bleeds red, white, and blue, one of his compatriots had angrily declared, "You better believe *I* bleed red, white, and blue, Bro."

Sands had dropped it. No sense getting in a fight over a song. But he was proven right several years later when the Stockdale presidential campaign made the song its unofficial anthem and The New Tomfools promptly sued, saying the song was against everything The New Freedom Party stood for. Sands had no idea how the dispute was worked out, but the campaign kept playing it, and now the song was associated with Stockdale as sure as "The Star-Spangled Banner" is associated with the Super Bowl. Funny how politicians can convince people of exactly the opposite of what's true. Funnier still, Sands thought, when we convince ourselves.

These thoughts buzzed in the back of Sands' mind like so many gnats, but the forefront of his attention was taken up with his new prison block-mate, Victoria Brzinski. She remained unconscious, strapped to the grate of her cell, her body slack, her head slumped forward and her hair spilling into her lap. He could just make out the side of her face, the slow rhythm of breath through her open mouth. How had the daughter of one of the most powerful men in the world been brought so low as to end up like this, in a place like *Inferno*? And why had she been placed in a cell directly opposite Sands? It was too fantastic to be a coincidence, but Sands could make no sense of it.

In the corridor, Ahmer continued to gape like he had never seen a woman before. Probably, Sands realized, he never had seen one like Victoria. Even in her comatose state—with her eyes empty slits, her face ashen, her lips almost blue—that avalanche of red hair seemed to glow of its own light.

"Do you—do you really know her, Sands?"

"Everybody knows her," Sands grumbled. "She's the Vice President's daughter."

"Of the United States, you mean."

"Yeah, that'd be the one."

Ahmer's head wagged as if the thought made him sad. "I don't follow politics."

But it wasn't through politics that Sands knew Victoria Brzinski. He had known her since long before the presidential campaign, going all the way back to his days at Stanford. At that time, Henry Brzinski was a professor of political science and a senior fellow at the Hoover Institution for War, Revolution, and Peace. The Doctor always insisted on referring to the institution by its full name, he said, to distinguish it from the "Hoover Institution of Vacuum Cleaners and Floor Sweepers." He was a star lecturer in the department, and his seminars on government were always filled to capacity.

Sands had missed the cut-off, but he managed to get in by simply having the temerity to knock at the office door of the Great Man himself and ask.

"I already have a hundred and fifty students," Brzinski said in reply to his request.

Brzinski didn't look Sands in the eye when he said this. Sitting behind a desk cluttered with musty-looking books and a menagerie of antique gewgaws and mementos, he had tried to give Sands the generic The-Great-Professor-

Deigns-to-Acknowledge-You glance, but the student's un-expected bulk stopped him. Brzinski blinked twice at the muscled torso in the black t-shirt, where gold letters spelling out "Money's Gym" were stretched like a pull of taffy. He raised his eyes briefly to Sands' face—verifying that there was indeed a face hovering above this mountain of flesh—and then contented himself with speaking to his belt buckle.

"Why should you," he said to the buckle, "be number one-fifty-one?"

"I've read your book," Sands said simply.

Brzinski smiled at some inner thought. "Which one?"

Sands hesitated, but he wouldn't be tripped up. He knew Brzinski had written only one actual book-length work—the rest were pamphlets and compilations. "The one where you say you won't be writing any more books. 'The Truth,' you said, 'is conveyed through living speech, not dead words on the page.'"

Brzinski nodded. "That will be an inconvenient quote when I decide to publish my memoirs."

Sands shrugged. Brzinski had lifted his gaze just high enough to catch it. "I guess a man of your stature ought to be entitled to write two. Books, I mean."

Brzinski didn't laugh or smile. Instead, he reached for a slip of paper and a pen. "I could quibble with your math, but I fear to further engage your formidable wit." He scribbled something and handed the paper to Sands. "Take this to the Registrar."

Sands thanked him, but Brzinski only replied that he should close the door on his way out.

From day one, it was obvious to Sands that Brzinski's seminar would be no run-of-the-mill course on American government. Having entered the classroom without a word of greeting, carrying no books, no notes, not so much as a roll sheet, the Doctor wrote on the white board: "Capital is the river on which all freedoms flow." He included the quotation marks, and like any good scholar, added his attribution: Henry U. Brzinski.

He didn't elucidate on what the "U" stood for. Instead, he paced back and forth, looking the students over like a general inspecting his troops. He didn't ask for quiet. He didn't have to. One by one, every student fell silent, mesmerized by his slow, pendulum-like movement. As abruptly as he had entered the room, he spoke: "George Washington said that government 'is force...It is a dangerous servant and a fearful master.'"

Pause.

"If you doubt that, ask anyone who has ever been audited by the IRS."

Polite laughter.

"And if you doubt that the Father of Our Country meant exactly what he said—if you doubt that our first Commander-in-Chief had any qualms about putting down any challenge to his authority—and I mean the authority to *tax* the citizenry for their hard-won capital—even if putting down that challenge meant personally leading an armed militia thirteen thousand strong against his fellow citizens, the very citizens who had voted him into office, the very citizens from whom his authority originated...Well. Then I invite you to look up a little incident known as The Whiskey Rebellion."

He added, "Not now."

The blonde seated next to Sands turned a brilliant red, as if Brzinski's laser eyes had the power to broil her like a lobster. Her guilty thumbs retreated from the keypad of her phone and curled into hiding. The phone itself leapt from her hands into her purse like a startled rat down a hole.

Sands always said it was in that moment that he fell in love with Carrie, but in truth, it was the moment after. With everyone around them laughing, the redhead sitting in front of Sands turned around and said, "Oh, my god—it had to be a blonde."

Although the words were cruel, Victoria Brzinski didn't say them with any particular malice. As Sands would learn, Dr. Brzinski's daughter simply had no filter. Or better to say, she *chose* to have no filter. She gave no quarter, but she expected none. Life was more fun that way.

If it had been the stereotypical case of a "sweet girl" being humiliated in class by a "mean girl" for the entertainment of her cynical, oh-so-hip peers, Sands was perfectly capable of choosing up sides and going into White Knight mode. But Carrie was a competitor, a cheerleader and athlete who knew what it was to fall on her face in front of a crowd. The redness that had glowed from neckline to scalp disappeared as quickly as it had emerged. She matched Victoria Brzinski smirk for smirk and turned her gaze right back at the professor, coolly waiting for him to continue. And it was in *that* moment that Sands really fell in love with Carrie.

After class, the snarky redhead turned to Sands again, held out her hand, and said, "Hi, I'm Victoria."

A lot of students—female students—had introduced themselves to Sands since his arrival at Stanford, but Victoria was the first to offer to shake his hand. Sands took it and replied in kind. And then, insinuating herself with a smooth, cocktail-party smile, the blonde held out her hand to the redhead and said, "Hi, I'm Carrie." She smiled at Sands, too, but they didn't shake, as if no introduction were necessary.

From that moment on, Sands and Carrie were a couple, with Victoria as frequent third wheel. "I didn't even get a say in the matter," Sands would joke later, when he told the story to friends. "It's like they looked at each other and said, 'Okay, he's with you.'"

But it wasn't that simple. Although Carrie and Victoria would tell anyone who asked that they were good friends, there was always an edge to the friendship. Of course, with Victoria, "edge" was a given, and if it ever seemed that the two women were in some kind of unspoken competition, Sands refused to accept the notion that he might be the prize.

A poor kid from the wrong side of 110th Street in lower Manhattan, Sands felt himself in heady company with two campus titans like Carrie and Victoria, the cheerleader and the professor's daughter. With his grades and athletic ability, Sands could have gotten a scholarship to any mid-level state school he wanted, but the elite schools were out of reach. The only way Sands could attend Stanford was on an ROTC scholarship, shuttling back and forth between Palo Alto and the University of Santa Clara campus where the program was located, working doubly hard to get all his coursework completed before the Army came calling for him to fulfill his end of the bargain—four years of active duty.

Sands had no particular desire at that time to make a career in the military. He had actually earned a walk-on role on the basketball team as a freshman, but when the coach offered him a full athletic scholarship, Sands hesitated. He had seen enough in the gyms and playgrounds of New York to know what an athletic scholarship usually meant: Four years of putting the classroom on the back burner for the team, after which the scholarship ran out and you were left to finish your degree on your own dime, wherever and whenever you could. At least with ROTC everything was paid for and you graduated on time.

As Sands considered his answer, the Coach asked him, "How many hours are you taking, Sands?"

"Nineteen, sir. That includes my ROTC lab."

"You'll need to cut back to fifteen. I know you want to graduate on time, but this is the Pac-10. We may not be UCLA, but we're a perennial contender, and that takes commitment. We'll redshirt you to give you an extra year. Now, I'm not promising you a lot of minutes. Maybe no minutes. That's up to you. But you'll be on the big stage."

"Can I think about it?"

The Coach told him he could. As it happened, it was Henry Brzinski that helped Sands make his decision.

-2-

There are two tragedies in life. One is not to get your heart's desire. The other is to get it.

—George Bernard Shaw

It was later that week. Sands was in Brzinski's class wearing his ROTC camo after a morning of drills. Brzinski was lecturing on his pet topic—the social contract between a government and its citizenry. As usual, he began with the concept of force.

"The only legitimate use of government force," he pronounced, "is the protection of our freedoms—not only from foreign terrorists but from domestic criminals as well. The worst kind of criminal is the thief. And the worst kind of thief is the unproductive citizen."

He let that sink in a moment. "How many of you are here on scholarship?"

The students exchanged uncomfortable glances. Brzinski never surveyed his students without leading up to some devastating point.

"Come now, a scholarship is something to be proud of. Let's see those hands."

A number of hands went up.

"Quite a few. Good. And how many receive grants of some sort?" More hands. "Student loans?" Many more hands. "So all but a handful of the one hundred, fifty-one students in this lecture hall receive some sort of financial aid. The rest of you, I presume, had the good fortune to be born to wealthy parents."

Chuckles from the room.

"And how many, out of all the students here, are paying the full cost of a Stanford University education, out of their own pockets?"

Not a single hand was raised.

"So, then. You are all receiving a handout, of one form or another." He raised his dark eyebrows, inviting anyone to quibble with him, but none took the bait. "So tell me, are these handouts charity, or must you repay them in some way?"

One student ventured that his student loans weren't charity. He would have to repay them, with interest.

"As you would a loan for a house, or a car." Brzinski stroked his chin with pretend thoughtfulness. "So an education is a product, and you pay for it like a product, is that it?"

The student supposed it was.

"In that case, like any product, it doesn't really matter who pays for it, as long as the bill gets paid. The same goes for government services, I suppose. You pay your taxes, you receive your services."

Many students agreed that was right.

"But some pay more taxes than others. Some pay no taxes at all. And yet we all enjoy the benefits of what government has to offer, more or less equally. We drive the same roads, we drink the same water, we enjoy the same protections from terrorists and foreign aggressors. What an arrangement! Imagine a restaurant—let's say a McDonald's—where everyone gets the same Big Mac, fries, and a Coke, but each pays a different amount, according to some arcane formula based on birth, race, gender, income, genetic deformity, and the federal tax code!"

He pointed. "Your Big Mac costs four dollars and fifty-nine cents. Yours costs three hundred dollars. Yours costs ten. And yours—because you don't have a job and can't get one because your mommy didn't love you and somebody in some other country was mean to your great-great-great-granddaddy three hundred years ago—your two all-beef patties and special sauce on a sesame seed bun is free."

There were a few chuckles here and there, but mostly an uncomfortable silence. One student held up his hand. "But isn't that the free enterprise system?"

"No! That's the 'freeloader-prize' system. The working men and women pay the bills. The freeloaders get the prizes."

At that moment, as she often did, Victoria turned round in her seat toward Sands and Carrie and mocked her father, screwing her face into a scowl and mouthing his words. Sands and Carrie were well practiced at keeping a stone face when Victoria went into one of her little performances, but when Sands saw the corner of Carrie's mouth twitch, a single laugh burst out of him like a stifled hiccup.

"You!" Brzinski thrust a finger straight at Sands. "Stand up."

Certain of an imminent dressing down, Sands got to his feet.

"How are you paying your tuition?"

"ROTC scholarship, sir."

"And how much is covered?"

"Everything."

"Everything. That should be adequate. Do you have to be special to earn that scholarship?"

"Sir?"

"Does it matter whether you are rich or poor, black or white, man or woman, Democrat or Republican? A descendent of the Saxe-Croburg-and-Gothas, perhaps? Is it open to anyone?"

"Anyone willing to work, sir."

"That's a novel idea. And who pays your tuition?"

"The government, sir."

"I think you mean the taxpayer, but we'll let that pass. And what do you have to do to repay this magnificent gift from your fellow citizens? Does it involve compound interest?"

"No, sir. Four years active duty, after I graduate."

"Service! You repay it with service!" Brzinski swept his gaze over the other students. "That is how a debt is paid, ladies and gentlemen. Not by getting a job. Not by making Mommy and Daddy proud. Not even by repaying loans. You repay a debt—a true debt—with service. And the surest and proudest service you can undertake is military service—the commitment to lay down your life for your fellow citizens, if need be. One student—one, in this entire class—has truly committed to serve. No doubt many of you think he is a fool to sign away four years of his life, but after those four years he will be a free, sovereign individual, beholden to no one. I wonder how many of the rest of you—with your student loans, credit cards, and thirty-year mortgages—will be able to say the same?"

Sands needed to hear no more. His decision was made. Basketball was out.

After class, Brzinski asked him to come to his office. Again, Sands thought he was in trouble, but before he could get the apology out of his mouth, the Doctor handed him a slip of paper. "That's my home address," he said. "I'd like you to come tonight. Cocktails at six-thirty, dinner at seven. No need to wear the uniform, but a tie would be appreciated."

Sands had no other plans, but Brzinski hadn't asked. He thanked him for the invitation and said he would be there.

It was an awkward affair from the beginning. When asked what he would like to drink, Sands unthinkingly said "Corona," just as if he had been in a bar. Brzinski didn't blink, but he had to call to the kitchen to get it, and Sands only realized his mistake when he saw everyone else sipping on ice-clear concoctions in martini glasses.

Although it was only a family dinner, it was quite formal, down to the uniformed maid who served it up, each course on a different plate. Dr. Brzinski sat at the head of a carved dining table, with Sands, as the guest of honor, at the opposite end. Victoria sat to Brzinski's right, her strange, brooding brother Todd—who had graduated the year before—to his left. Brzinski's wife—who the Doctor had introduced simply as "My wife"—sat at Sand's elbow, seldom speaking and watching him with bird-like eyes.

Brzinski conducted the dinner like a symposium—introducing topics, soliciting opinions, offering counterarguments and pronouncements covering every-thing from the latest Supreme Court decision to the qual-ity of the veal. Todd engaged his father most vigorously, with a nervous edge to his voice and a look in his dark eyes that was at once angry and fearful. Victoria was unusually subdued, parrying her father's forays only when she was directly addressed. Instead of the usual sardonic quips delivered with a spark in her eye, she affected boredom. Sands had never seen, or even imagined, Victoria embarrassed by anything, but he wondered if her exaggerated disinterest weren't just a cover.

After dinner, Sands was invited into Brzinski's study, where the Doctor poured brandy and offered cigars. Sands took the brandy, but demurred on the smoke.

Brzinski's study was like his school office, only more so. Among the items that crammed the shelves and hung from the paneled walls were a Knights Templar shield and sword, a boar's head, an Indian lance, a flintlock rifle, and a tricorn hat. On his cluttered desk was a crystal pyramid topped with an all-seeing eye, what appeared to be a loaded revolver, and a strange object like a ball of endless, interwoven triangles, which Sands vaguely recognized from high school geometry as a "600-cell."

"Have a seat." Brzinski indicated the two leather captain's chairs that sat before his desk.

"Thank you, sir."

Instead of taking the chair next to Sands, or the high-backed swivel chair opposite, Brzinski sat on the edge of the desk. It gave him a friendly, almost fatherly, aspect, but it also allowed him to look down at Sands rather than up. He picked up a folder, leafed through a handful of papers, and pulled one out.

Sands guessed it was his final paper, an in-depth research project he had written with Victoria. He had wanted to work with Carrie, but the partnerships were "randomly" assigned by alphabetical opposite, so that Zacarro was paired with Adams, Wilson with Armstrong, and so on. As luck would have it, Simon matched up with Brzinski, although Sands wondered if luck had anything to do with it.

"You're mine, sucker!" Victoria had bragged when the assignments were posted. Carrie was paired with a pimply faced munchkin named Marvin Morton (or was it Morton Marvin?) whose idea of eye contact was to stare at her breasts. Sands tried to soften the blow by suggesting that they could all work together in the library, but the munchkin rejected that, insisting that it would just be a distraction, since each team would be working on a different topic.

"Marvin's wise to us, Sands," Victoria said. "He knows we just want to steal his ideas."

It was all a great joke to Victoria. Sands dreaded the long study sessions the project would require—hours with the two of them together, hours apart from Carrie. But Victoria had a brilliant mind, and although she had a tendency to drift off task, she was a font of ideas and had an intuitive grasp of how to shape them. During their study sessions she could be teasing—sometimes obnoxiously so—but Sands was relieved that she was never flirty. Carrie wasn't the jealous type, but sometimes Sands could feel her eyes on them when they happened to be in the library at the same time. He wanted to tell her that Victoria had given her no reason for jealousy, but he realized that would only make the situation worse. In time, he became so engrossed in the project that the hours flew by without him even giving Carrie a thought.

"Truly excellent work, Sands." Brzinski held the paper, staring down his nose at the title through black-rimmed reading glasses.

"Thank you, sir. It's really just based on your ideas. And I have to give most of the credit to Victoria."

"Most? I doubt that."

Before Sands could protest, Brzinski said, "You and my daughter make a good team."

"Yes, sir. She's a very . . . interesting person. Really brilliant."

"She's creative but directionless," Brzinski pronounced, dropping the paper onto the desktop. "You're unimaginative but disciplined. Together, you could go far. With, ah, my support, of course."

"I, uh..."

"You don't find her attractive?"

Sands set his brandy snifter on the desk. "Sir, I'm engaged to Carrie McKee. We're going to marry when I enlist."

Brzinski nodded. "A sweet girl for a good soldier. I would have thought you'd aim higher."

Sands felt the color rising to his cheeks. "Higher than love?"

Brzinski affected his best fatherly smile, took a stroll around his desk and sat in his chair. It seemed to be on a raised platform—he sat almost eye to eye with Sands.

"Love is a practice, my boy, not a goal. It's a discipline. Sometimes a tool."

Sands frowned, trying to follow.

"I've upset you."

"No, sir. It's just—"

"No matter. I have a vision for the future, Sands. Some will have a place in it. Some won't. A young man with your drive and intelligence can always make a place for himself."

He slid the paper across the desk, a gesture of dismissal. Sands stared at the title, the pride he had felt in crafting it suddenly deflated:

Prisoners at Sea Secured:
A Modest Proposal for a Maritime Penal System.

-3-

What a heavy burden is a name that has become too famous.

—Voltaire

Sands sat in his prison cell: the place he had made for himself.

The video feed was on, and a news anchor sat before a map of the Koreas, a shaded area just north of the border marked "Oil Fields."

"Although South Korea denies the charge," the anchor was saying, "North Korean President Kim Jong-Seung is accusing the South of using their superior drilling technology to steal the oil from under his feet. President Stockdale has reached out to China to help mediate the dispute..."

The anchor spoke in a heightened voice, matching his verbal tension to the political tension in the region, but Sands paid little attention. Instead, he kept his eyes on Victoria, still sitting with her back to the grate of her cell, still no more than half-conscious, the straps around her torso holding her upright. Seeing her in this way, in this place, had been a shock, and it made him see his surroundings with a clarity he hadn't since he had first laid eyes on the ship.

"In a bizarre development, Radwan Karga of Bashkiristan is attempting to stir the pot in his on-going vendetta against the United States..."

The mention of Karga got Sands' attention, and he looked up at the monitor to see the familiar face, with its black unibrow like a second mustache, mouthing threats from the balcony of his presidential palace. At least it looked like a balcony, but there was something suspicious about the way the video of Karga didn't quite match the video of the crowd he supposedly addressed. Rumor was that Karga's fear of drone strikes kept him strictly out of the open air, and that his balcony speeches were actually delivered from a digitized set in some underground bunker. Nevertheless, he always put on a good show.

"Let the American criminals be warned: I will stand with my brother Kim. Your money and oil cannot shield you from a nuclear dagger!"

It was the same old threat Karga had been making since Sands and his team had taken out the installation on the Caspian. If this new "alliance" between Islamist Bashkiristan and Communist North Korea was absurd, it was also familiar in a tactical sense. It was just Karga once again attempting to play one against the other, attaching himself like a lamprey to the shark of the moment, sucking up what scraps of advantage he could, ready to jump free the moment the shark got the fisherman's gaff.

"The power is the six hundred."

Sands heard the words clearly, low and distinct. But they hadn't come from the video feed, and the voice didn't sound like any of his male block-mates.

"Victoria?"

She was stirring, her head rotating in a tight, languid circle, as if her half-open eyes were following the flight of a swirling mite of dust.

"The power," she repeated, but the words that followed were unintelligible. She muttered on, her volume rising and falling, her words slurred, then clear, then slurred again. "The power...the six hundred...not the party...the six hundred...the power...."

"Victoria, can you hear me?"

Sands rattled the grate of his cage, shouted her name. Victoria's speech only became more erratic, her breathing more labored.

Then she stopped.

"Victoria! Victoria, talk to me!"

She gasped, sputtered out a few more words. Like a struggling swimmer, she gulped at the air, her arms straining at her bonds.

"What is it, Sands?" Rashid called from the neighboring cell.

"I don't know. She needs help."

Sands stepped back from the grate to the center of his cell and stared hard at the monitor. He waved his arms, made a choking motion with his hands around his throat, and pointed emphatically toward Victoria's cell.

Ahmer, ever watchful, got the message. From his post in the Vestibule, he grabbed his pack and headed for the hatch, moving like someone following an irresistible urge.

Oleg stood up, ready to block his way. "Where are you going?"

"Gotta get to the head."

"With that?" He pointed at Ahmer's pack.

Ahmer opened it to reveal a clutch of comic books. "Reading materials." He screwed up his face. "I gotta go!"

"All right, all right."

Knowing Oleg would be watching, Ahmer went straight to the head and pretended to lock himself in a stall, the only place where, in theory, anyone on *Inferno* could expect privacy. He had chosen the stall nearest the air vent, which he had previously rigged for easy removal. Taking advantage of a blind spot he had spotted after weeks of meticulous searching, he slid under the partition, lifted the register free, and slipped into the vent, pulling the register back into place after him. It only required a few feet of crab-walking to get to the main ventilator shaft, from which he could access any deck. All the air shafts were monitored, too, though, and because they were restricted areas, Ahmer knew if he were spotted there he would have no plausible cover for his actions. He switched over to the service shaft stairwell, which guards and even Drones used whenever they were more convenient than the elevators. The diversion with the head had only been to throw off Oleg. Once Ahmer felt sure he wasn't being actively watched, he could blend in with the usual crew traffic, knowing that even if he were spotted, most of his fellow Drones wouldn't rat him out.

As Ahmer approached Sands' cell, he could hear the big man rattling his grate, and for a moment he feared Sands had gone psycho.

"Ahmer!"

"I'm here."

"She's having trouble breathing. Can you get those restraints off her?"

"They took the chip. Without it I can't get in."

"You got a knife?"

"A knife?"

"A knife! A knife! To cut the straps!"

"Knives are contraband."

Victoria's head snapped back against the grate. Her chest heaved with a great gasp rattling deep in her throat, and she went still.

"She's fading," Sands said. "Every time she does that, it's longer between breaths."

Ahmer produced a hypodermic from his pack. "This might help."

"What is it?"

"Our own concoction. The Techs, I mean. Fluorenol, phytochemicals, B-vitamins, biphetamine, I think, and uh...One more ingredient...It's um—"

"Just tell me what it does."

"It wakes you up."

Sands looked at Victoria. She was still as death. Thirty-five seconds since her last breath. Forty.

"Give it to her."

Ahmer held the hypo up to the dim light, squeezed the plunger until a thread of liquid spurted from the needle. He bent to the grate, searching for a spot between the steel that lined up with a vulnerable area in Victoria's restraints.

"Hurry up!"

"It's not easy. I need to find a vein."

"Her neck, Ahmer, try her neck."

"Okay, I found a spot." He threaded the needle through carefully, having found a space in the grate that lined up with his target. "I have to be careful not to break it," he explained, as he slowly pushed the needle in. Sands grimaced as he watched the long sliver of steel slide into Victoria's neck. "Okay, here goes." Ahmer thumbed the plunger forward until the hypo was empty. He withdrew the needle quickly, as if he expected some violent reaction.

For a moment, there was nothing. Then Victoria gasped, flailed her legs out, pounded her heels against the deck, and bucked against her restraints till Sands thought she would pull the steel grate from its welds. In a moment it was over. Her breathing returned, raspy but steady.

"Adrenaline," Ahmer said brightly. "That was the other ingredient. Adrenaline."

Sands gave him a withering look.

"Where am I?"

Victoria's voice was so faint it was barely audible. Sands wasn't sure he had heard her.

"Did she say something?"

"She ask where is she."

Sands pressed against the grate, getting as close to her as he could. "Victoria, it's Sands. Sands Simon. You're in a prison cell."

"The six hundred cell."

"You're on a prison ship. *The Inferno.*"

She began muttering—like before, but more fluidly.

"The power is the six hundred...not the party...not the president...the power...the power is the six hundred..."

"Victoria, I can't understand you."

Her muttering came quicker, her words jumbling into nonsense as her voice rose in volume and pitch. In the torrent of gibberish, the number six-hundred was repeated again and again. Sands had never heard Victoria's voice like this before, as if another being had taken it over. Yet there was something strangely familiar about it.

He looked at Ahmer. The young Pakistani had backed away from the cell, his eyes staring.

"Ahmer, what is it?"

Ahmer pointed. "The spot on her wrist."

Sands looked. Victoria had managed to free one of her arms. It was at her side, the wrist exposed. Sands saw a faint, blue-black smudge.

"It's a birthmark," he said. "She's always had it."

Ahmer shook his head. He pulled a pen-like device from his pack and directed a beam of invisible ultraviolet light through the grate. When the beam fell onto Victoria's wrist, the mark leapt to life, projecting a three-dimensional hologram of a complex geometric figure.

It was a holo-tat. Sands had seen one or two of them in the service. They were too expensive for government pay—three or four paychecks for something the size of a thimble. And under anything but UV light they didn't look like much but a smudge of ink. Sands supposed they could be spectacular at a disco, bouncing in the dark from the bodies of a hundred gyrating dancers. Only rich hipsters got them. And the occasional Marine.

Ahmer stared at the image hovering three inches above Victoria's wrist, transfixed by its multicolored, interwoven angles.

"The 600-cell."

But Sands was no longer looking at the holographic image. He was looking instead at Victoria's smudged wrist, remembering the first time he had seen such a mark. He was transported back to Bashkiristan, to the hapless operative of Karga's covert mint. Just before the mysterious spook they called Spear shot him, the operative had pulled back his shirtsleeve to reveal a "birthmark" that looked exactly like Victoria's. "See?" he had said to G.K. "Like you."

"She shouldn't be here," Ahmer said.

As if in reply, Victoria erupted with a stream of syllables too structured and inflected to be called gibberish. And that, too, clicked in Sands' mind, conjuring forth the image of Bloodyface, the rapt giant speaking in tongues just before his death.

Ahmer backed up, fear in his eyes, until he hit the bulkhead. With a glance at Sands, he ran.

"Ahmer! Ahmer, come back here!"

But he was gone, leaving Sands alone to witness Victoria's mad raving.

But not alone.

"Someone," Rashid said, his voice drifting to Sands' ears from the next cell, "is speaking to God."

-4-

Courage is the price that life exacts for granting peace.
—Amelia Earhart

Three-and-a-half-year-old Emanuel stood next to his mother, using her lap to hold the picture book he was reading. Carrie stroked his hair with one hand, thumbing through a fat folder with the other, checking again that she hadn't gotten any of her papers mixed in with Emanuel's stack of coloring and story books. During their three-hour wait, Emanuel had gone from fidgety, to cranky, to sleepy, and back to fidgety again. Rick wasn't much better. He sat with his shoulders hunched, legs crossed at the knees, fanning one dangling foot in the air like a dog with an itch.

Carrie put a hand to Rick's knee and squeezed until the foot went still.

"Sorry."

Rick uncrossed his legs and slouched down into his chair, a mismatched plastic companion to Carrie's. They had uneven legs and poorly contoured backs that seemed designed to aggravate a tired lumbar region. Carrie wanted to tell him to sit up straight—and take off those ridiculous aviator sunglasses. He was wearing sweats and sneakers, trying to look as unmilitary as possible, but in his brush-cut and aviators he looked exactly like what he was—a Fed, a cop, an officer, a by-the-book square out of place among the unwashed rabble.

They were at the makeshift headquarters of the Washington bureau of Justice International, a grassroots activist organization derided among its detractors as "Greenpeace with Guns" for the actions of some of its militant associates. The headquarters was housed in an old warehouse, its thirty-foot ceiling looming darkly above a hundred open cubicles huddled in the center of the vast concrete floor. The surrounding wall was lined with folding chairs, where Carrie and Rick and Emanuel had waited with dozens of other families, mostly poor, mostly immigrants or the children of immigrants, speaking a Babel of different tongues, but all there for the same reason— someone they loved was among the "disappeared," the countless thousands of criminals, refugees, and "undesirables" who had been arrested and sent to prison, never to be heard from again.

Carrie's number had finally been called, and after another hour of questionnaires and interviews, they sat before a metal desk with chipped enamel paint that looked like a castoff from some 1950s-era secretarial pool. The desk was stacked high with accordion folders and legal briefs, some of which had spilled onto the seat of the ratty swivel chair that sat behind it. There was no other furniture. Hundreds of other files were stacked in storage boxes that lined the thin cubicle walls like the earthworks of a Spanish fortress.

Carrie noticed Rick peeking over the top of his aviators at a banner that hung from the ceiling. It read: JUSTICE INTERNATIONAL INNOCENCE PROJECT.

"Innocence." Rick curled his lip. "That's a laugh."

Carrie cut him a look. "You're supposed to be his defense attorney."

"*Was* his defense attorney." He shook his head at the floor. "If the JAG gets wind of me being here I'll need my own defense attorney."

"Honestly, Rick, you act like these people are criminals."

"They're *terrorists!*"

A young man in a blue sport coat and tie at war with rumpled khakis and jogging shoes appeared behind him.

"Actually, we're lawyers, Major Guidry. Just like you."

"How'd you know my name?"

Carrie couldn't help but feel disgusted by the panic in Rick's voice. The J.I. counsel opened the file he was carrying and produced a dossier paper-clipped with a photo of Rick in his dress uniform. "You were Captain Simon's legal counsel, I believe?"

Rick slumped back into his chair, looking and feeling foolish.

The counsel cleared a spot for himself and sat down, spreading the file out onto his desk. "Quite a body of evidence against the captain." He picked up a photo, grimaced, and turned it over. To Carrie he said, "And what's your relation?"

"He's my son's father."

Emanuel looked up from his book, first at Carrie, then at Rick. Rick reached over and mussed his hair.

"I see." The counsel flipped the rest of the papers in the file into one stack and closed the folder over them. "Well, despite that banner, we don't make judgments about guilt or innocence here."

"That's convenient."

"Habeas corpus, Counselor." He gestured at the stacks of files around him. "We've got thousands of claims of false imprisonment. Some complaints may be legitimate. Some may not. But they don't mean a thing if we can't even prove the person—or the prison—exists."

"You see?" Rick looked at Carrie like he'd just won an argument. "Conspiracy theories. Invisible prisons. Black Rafts. Maybe Sands was abducted by aliens."

"Rick, you're not helping."

As the silence stretched between them, Emanuel held up his picture book for Rick to see. "Daddy, horsey. See, Daddy. Horsey."

"I see, son." Rick picked him up and sat him on his knee.

"Lion!" Emanuel pointed at another picture.

"That's good, Emanuel. Let the grownups talk a minute, okay?"

The counsel pulled a grainy photo from his desk and held it up, using his pen as a pointer. "This is a satellite image of what we believe is a black raft in the Sea of Japan."

"How did you get that?" Rick demanded.

"Illegally, Major. Would you like me to tell you more?"

His silence indicated he would not.

"Ms. Guidry, I can't promise you anything about your case. Frankly, we don't have the resources to investigate a quarter of the cases that come to us. But I can tell you, with high confidence, that very soon we will have hard proof of the government's secret prison program."

"What does that mean?"

"It means that if Captain Sands is one of the 'disappeared,' his chances of reappearing are about to go up."

-5-

Don't be humble; you're not that great.

— Golda Meir

Vice President Brzinski sat on a leather sofa in what his staff called "the screening room"—a partitioned area of his office in the West Wing—scanning a bank of six video monitors. All but one were muted, and Brzinski had his eyes fixed on that one as if it had just called him a dirty name.

On the monitor, an anchorwoman furrowed her botoxed brow with journalistic seriousness as she sat before a stock image of a man gripping the bars of his prison cell and staring forlornly into space. The punning caption asked: "PASS-port to Nowhere?"

"In a statement released just hours ago, Justice International—the activist group President Stockdale has characterized as 'terrorists with legal briefs'—claims to have located one of the rumored secret prison ships known as 'black rafts' off the coast of South Korea."

The image shifted to a grainy satellite photo similar to the one the JI legal counsel had shown Carrie and Rick. Brzinski's eyes flitted quickly to the other monitors, several of which featured the same image.

"Along with their statement," the reporter continued, "Justice International released this photograph, which appears to be a satellite image of a large container ship. JI offered no further proof of the ship's nature or location, nor anything to verify the image's authenticity. They do claim, however, to have dispatched a flotilla of boats to intercept the ship and provide first-hand—"

Brzinski snuffed the six video eyes with an angry thrust of his remote and turned to his chief aide and bodyguard, the man known as "Spear."

"We've got a leak."

Spear, who had a habit of standing at rigid attention, even when he was in his civilian dress of black suit and tie, gave a single shake of his head. "I don't think so, sir. That so-called satellite image is laughable."

"And yet they seem to know the location of one of our ships. 'Sea of Japan, off the coast of South Korea'—that's not a guess."

"No, sir."

"How did they find it? These things are supposed to be invisible."

"Invisible to radar, sir. Not invisible."

Brzinski fixed Spear with a look so dark it rattled his normally unshakeable military cool.

"Don't bandy words with me, boy."

"No, sir."

The voice of Brzinski's secretary came over the intercom. Her tone conveyed as much as she dared of the impatience of a thrice-repeated request. "Sir, the President is waiting."

"Let him wait!"

Spear kept his counsel. His respect for the wrath of the Vice President outweighed his respect for the chain of command. Besides, he could see that Brzinski was hatching a plan. The downward wedge of his dark eyebrows breached and he looked at Spear with something akin to a twinkle.

"It seems we have the proverbial two birds to kill."

Spear nodded his understanding. "With one very big stone?"

***

In the Oval Office, President Stockdale stared glumly at the unsigned order that lay on his desk. His inaugural Bible and gun were at his elbow—the double comfort he carried with him everywhere he went. The gun was loaded. The Secret Service didn't like it, but what the Secret Service liked or didn't like carried little weight in Stockdale's administration. They were more like event planners now. They provided logistics, but Spear and his Force guard, always in their distinctive black camo, provided the real security. As rigid and upright as the flags that flanked the President's desk, they stood silent sentinel to even the most top secret discussions.

The President sighed. He was surrounded by Brzinski, Secretary of Defense "Mal" Mallory, and Secretary of State Ken Lum, who all pressed around him as if physically urging him to put pen to paper.

"But how do we drop a nuke in the Sea of Japan without killing people—that's what I want to know."

"Mr. President, I can't promise we won't lose a fishing boat or two..." Brzinski smiled at the possibility like it was some amusing fancy. "But those are acceptable losses against all-out nuclear war."

"But won't we be *starting* a nuclear war?"

"Preempting one," Brzinski explained with a teacher's patience. "And besides, *we* won't be the ones starting it."

Stockdale turned to the secretary of Defense. "Mal, are you on board with this? Won't North Korea retaliate?"

"They'll never get the chance," Mallory said. "The second the missile launches, President Park will blame Kim—"

"Now, Park," the President interrupted, "he's our guy, right?"

Mallory's lips stretched into a taught line, but his tone remained even. "Yes, he's the president of *South* Korea. We immediately confirm his claim about the launch. While Kim—that's the president of *North* Korea—"

"I know who Kim is, dammit!"

"Of course, sir. Kim's first instinct will be to denounce his accusers. But while he's making his denials, we'll already be taking out his nuclear arsenal."

Stockdale pondered deeply. "So it's a pretext."

The others exchanged glances, but no one spoke. Best to let the President work out whatever he could for himself.

"But what about China and Russia? Won't they know we launched first?"

"The fog of war, sir," Lum offered. "I can assure you that no matter the facts on the ground, politically—where the real decisions are made—these matters are always up for interpretation."

Stockdale slapped his desk. "But dang it, how do we know Kim even plans to attack? Where's the evidence?"

"What kind of evidence would you like, Mr. President? A mushroom cloud?"

Brzinski had a knack for saying the most awful things in the most pleasant way. It made Stockdale angry, but he never knew quite how to address it.

"Don't get dramatic."

Brzinski leaned in confidentially, his tone quiet, but plain for all to hear. "Mr. President, there is an untapped reservoir of two hundred billion barrels of oil on the Korean Peninsula. The question you have to ask yourself is this: Is it going to be controlled by the leader of the free world—or a cartoon dictator in high heels?"

Stockdale stewed a moment as all eyes—even those of Spear and his guard—were upon him. He reached for his pen.

-6-

Only the guy who isn't rowing has time to rock the boat.
—Jean Paul Sartre

Sands was sitting in the lotus position in the center of his cell, just finishing his meditation, when the monitor came on for its morning broadcast. First, it was some inane cartoon in Spanish. It didn't seem too funny to Sands, but he heard idiot laughter from a few of the other cells in the block. After that, a dramatic headline announced "Breaking News," but instead of a news anchor speaking in dramatic tones directly into the camera, the image was of President Stockdale sitting at his desk in the Oval Office, apparently reading his inaugural Bible.

In one of those phony TV moments in which the person on screen pretends the camera is some unannounced visitor, Stockdale looked up, grunted a good-morning, and closed his book. He set the Bible aside, placed his trusty pistol upon it, and looked into the camera.

Sands shook his head. What an act.

"My fellow Americans—and to all freedom-loving people around the world—just an hour ago, in an unprovoked attack on a peaceful neighbor, North Korean Dictator Kim Jong-Seung launched a nuclear missile at South Korea. Fortunately, that missile landed harmlessly in the Sea of Japan..."

"Bullshit."

The single word from Victoria's cell was soft but clear. Sands bounced to his feet and went to the grate. "Victoria! It's Sands. Do you recognize me?"

Victoria's face turned in the direction of Sands' voice. She could barely hold her head up. Her eyes were slits, the corners of her lashes caked together. Her partially free arm moved spasmodically.

"Don't struggle. You're in restraints."

"Sands?"

"That's right. Sands Simon. Your old Stanford buddy."

A faint smile played across her dry lips. "Imagining things."

"No, Victoria, it's really me. Victoria!"

He called her name a few more times, but she was out again. On the overhead monitor, the President droned on.

"That's why, as I speak, our bombers are taking out Kim's nuclear threat. The United States of America will not stand idly by as our allies—"

The screen went to static. The monitor remained on, but nothing was being broadcast.

"This is new," Sands said to no one.

He was about to whack the side of the monitor with his hand, but he heard inmates up and down the cell block doing just that. So it wasn't just his monitor. Confusion and anger echoed all around him. The inmates did not like having their allotment of video entertainment interrupted.

Somewhere on Top-deck a siren sounded. There was a deep rumble below decks, and a moment of frightening silence.

"Sands," Rashid called to him. "Sands, what's happening?"

"I don't know. A storm maybe?"

A brilliant flash of light penetrated the ship, all the way to deck nine. For a moment, Sands was dazzled, as when the lights in the arena blazed up before Battle. This was no storm, he told himself, and that was no lightning flash. Sands stood in the center of his cell, his stance wide, his senses at full alert. From the next cell, he could hear Rashid praying in Arabic. Except for Rashid, the ship was dead silent, and with sixty-thousand other souls, Sands waited for whatever would come next.

The thunder of a thousand freight trains shuddered through the ship's steel hull. The deck beneath Sands' feet pitched violently, and he was thrown against the grate. With a terrifying groan, the ship listed to the port side, farther and farther, until it was near rolling over. The stern simultaneously made a backward slide down some great swell, sending the deck into a slow, sickening spin.

Twining his fingers through the grate, Sands held on as best he could. Either the ship would continue to list until it flipped, or it would roll back upright. Either way, he was in for a ride.

Screams, sirens, the thud of tumbling bodies filled his ears. He shouted to Victoria, but she was oblivious, her head lolling about under her long red mane as her torso was held fast to the grate by her restraints.

The ship did not roll over. Just as Sands' feet were losing their purchase on the deck, the ship stopped listing, rolled back in the opposite direction, and then rocked itself upright.

The lights had gone out, replaced by the feeble, greenish glow of the auxiliaries. From somewhere far above, Top-deck perhaps, Sands thought he could hear gunshots, maybe chopper blades. It was difficult to make out anything clearly in the din made by the terrified inmates.

In the next cell, Sands could tell that Rashid was prostrate, praying. Victoria was out. He could make out a few others cowering in their cells like frightened children. Sands grabbed the grate of his cell and rattled it with all his might, but nothing budged. It was intact. No stress points, no weaknesses were apparent to him.

There was no mistaking it now. He could hear explosions from above. It sounded like a battle was being waged. If the ship were to go down, he would have less chance than a rat.

The grate was too strong to be breached with just his hands and feet. Sands surveyed his cell, looking for anything that could be used as a tool, a weapon, any point of weakness that might be exploited. He turned a malevolent eye on the steel toilet. It burbled with brown insolence. He attacked it with everything he had, kicking it, wrenching it, pulling on it, but the welds held firmly. In a rage now, he picked up his food tray, and holding it like a shield against his forearm he charged against the grate, bashing it again and again until he fell to his knees in exhaustion.

Two hours later, Sands was again sitting in the center of his cell—not meditating, just staring into the semi-darkness. The ship was stable now. The sounds of guns and helicopters had ceased, and the inmates were relatively quiet. The rumble of the engines and the churn of the great propellers could be heard, below and aft, in their ceaseless turning, a sign that the ship was still operational, even if not quite back to normal. There was nothing to do but wait.

Sands heard the scrape of a sandal on the deck, and two eyes appeared, glowing like pinholes in a feeble shaft of light.

"Helter Skelter."

Sands, who had trained himself to manifest a meditative state, even in pitched battle, nearly jumped out of his skin.

"Jesus! Are you trying to scare me?"

The figure moved closer in the light. It was Ahmer.

"It's helter skelter."

Sands got up and went to the grate.

"You've got to help us, Sands. It's helter skelter. All is helter skelter."

"Ahmer, I swear, if you speak the title of my least favorite Beatles song one more time, I'll—"

But looking into Ahmer's face, he swallowed his threat. Sands had seen enough in war to know what real fear looked like.

"What is it, Ahmer? What's happening?"

"They left us. The Captain, the Warden, the guards. They all left. You've got to help us."

"Help who?"

"The Techs."

"The..." Sands laughed. "You mean the Drones? You want me to help the Drones? The little creepy-crawlies that are always buzzing around watching everything we do?"

"I can get you out." Ahmer pulled from his pack the electronic hand device that served as a key to all the cell hatches.

Sands' interest was piqued, but he wanted to know more. "Why did the guards leave?"

"The war."

"Korea?"

Ahmer nodded.

"What's that got to do with us?"

"I told you, it's hel— Everything is chaos. The whole world."

Sands doubted that. Maybe the conflict had spread, but if it had been global nuclear war they wouldn't be talking right now.

"Why didn't the crew take you with them?"

"They say they will come back, but we don't believe them. Like you say—we're just Drones."

Sands nodded at the hatch.

"So open it."

"You promise to help?"

"Open it." Sands' tone made clear it wasn't a suggestion.

Ahmer fingered the keypad on his device. The indicator light on the hatch turned from green to red, and the latch popped. Sands pushed the hatch open and stepped through, Ahmer cringing back from him. It was the first time since *Inferno* had been commissioned that an inmate had been outside his cell without restraints and a squad of armed guards.

Sands nodded at Victoria's cell. "Hers too."

Ahmer took another step back. "I can't. They took the chip. You saw they took it."

Sands shoved Ahmer against the bulkhead, one massive forearm pressed against his windpipe.

"Do not fuck with me, Ahmer. Unless you want to die, you open that hatch. Understand?"

Ahmer managed a nod, and Sands released the pressure. Ahmer reached into his pack, and Sands snatched it from him with snake-like quickness. He rummaged through it, satisfying himself that Ahmer had not secreted some weapon before handing it back.

Ahmer found an inner pocket, unzipped it, and produced a ring, like a keyring, with multiple chips attached to it.

"You tricky little bastard."

Ahmer managed the slightest of smiles as he selected a chip and inserted it into his tablet. His fingers danced over the keypad, and in a moment, Victoria's cell was open. Sands clambered in, unfastened Victoria's restraints, and carried her out. Her eyes fluttered, but she was in no condition to walk.

"All right, let's go."

"Sands!" Rashid called out to him. "Sands, take me with you!"

Sands looked at him, for the first time getting a good look at the slight, bearded man with the swept-back silver hair. Rashid pleaded with his eyes as Sands weighed the angles. Already the other inmates were taking up the call to be freed.

"We have to go," Ahmer said.

Rashid looked at Victoria. Her face was flushed, her eyes darting sightlessly, like one having a dream.

"On the outside I was a doctor," he said. "I can help with the girl."

Sands nodded for Ahmer to open Rashid's cell. Ahmer's eyes sounded silent alarms, but he obeyed without comment.

The moment Rashid was out, the clamor around them increased, spreading from cell to cell throughout the block: "Me too, Sands! Open up! Let me out!"

Ahmer looked at Sands in terror, fearing the order he was certain would come. But Sands just stepped aside and indicated for Ahmer to lead the way. The young Pakistani hurried toward the main elevator, Rashid close behind. Before Sands followed after them he favored his fellows with a smile and said, "Sorry guys. Catch you on the other side."

·7·

It is the old practice of despots to use a part of the people to keep the rest in order.

—Thomas Jefferson

The jeers and thrown debris of Sands' block-mates were just a taste of the bedlam that followed him and his unusual party as they made their slow ascent from Treachery to Limbo deck. The main elevator was an open cage that put them on display for anyone with an eye-line, and the sight of two unshackled inmates and a woman being led by an unarmed Drone generated more excitement than a battle royal in the arena. Sands could feel the furor building as the gossip mill ginned up, rumors forming and spreading through the ship like ripples over still water.

"Next time," Sands remarked to Ahmer, "we take the back stairs."

When Ahmer opened the hatch that led to the Top-deck, Sands and Rashid were staggered by the dazzling sunlight. Sands let Victoria's feet fall to the deck as one hand reflexively went up to shield his eyes. Almost as shocking to their systems, after years of being locked up inside a reverberating tin can, was the natural quiet and freshness of the open air. As their eyes and ears adjusted, they could see the blue of the sky, hear the waves and sea-gulls, feel the cool air against their skins and in their lungs.

Ahmer was eager to get to the Vestibule, but he gave the two men their moment. They each leaned back against the bulkhead, their eyes squinted against the glare, their faces lifted to the sun. Just listening. Just feeling. But their blissful moment was brief. When their eyes had adjusted enough that they could fully open them and look around, they saw the wreckage of a Marine helicopter burning on the flight deck, and in the distance, the towering remnants of a mushroom cloud.

"I told you," Ahmer said. "The world is gone crazy."

Ahmer led them across a space of open deck to the recessed entrance to the Vestibule, situated like a dank basement to the airy, glassed-in expanse of the Command Deck above it. As far as Sands could tell, the Command Deck was deserted, as was the entire upper deck of the ship. It was eerie to see such a big space so empty of people. Ahmer rapped at the hatch of the Vestibule three times—one long, two short—and waited expectantly for the lock to turn. But the signal didn't take. From inside, a muffled voice said, "Is that you, Ahmer?"

Ahmer stepped back, looked up at the surveillance camera perched above the recess, and held up his hands in annoyance.

And these are the guys, Sands thought, who are the brains of the ship's security system.

The hatch opened, and they stepped inside, the dim interior a welcome relief to Sands' and Rashid's smarting eyes. The place was a hacker's paradise—jam-packed with monitors, keyboards, and all sorts of electronic equipment, some original, but some obviously improvised by the tech-savvy Drones. The set-up was two concentric hexagons—a central command unit with six swivel seats and wrap-around consoles that represented the Drones' individual work stations—and the interior wall, where there were more graphic displays, work benches, storage cabinets, and tool racks. Every available surface was piled with hacker flotsam and jetsam—decommissioned CPUs, joysticks, cables, headsets, game pieces, and food containers. There were no windows—unless they were hidden behind the dart board or the Bollywood movie posters. Two details that caught Sands' eye were an alcove with two cots and what looked like a stocked snack bar.

Sands took all this in with a glance, and dismissed it. His attention was focused instead on the Drones. There were five of them—four males and, to Sands' surprise, one female. Like Ahmer, they were all kids, the oldest no more than twenty. And also like him, they were all terrified. Sands knew instantly that it had been Ahmer's idea to bring him there, and that it was only out of desperation that the others had agreed. If Ahmer had sold Sands as their potential savior, his comrades weren't yet ready to buy into him as more than a proven threat. They stood back from the hatch in a semi-circle, fear in their eyes and weapons in hand. But not real weapons. Just whatever they had been able to scrounge—kitchen knives, a hammer, a table leg.

The biggest of them—a scowling, buzz-cut blond who looked like he might have been familiar with the inside of a gym—sized up the situation and gaped at Ahmer in anger.

"Jesus, Ahmer, you said you were bringing *one!*"

Ahmer cut his eyes at Sands but said nothing.

"We're a package deal," Sands said. Without taking his eyes off the big kid, he kicked a pile of junk out of a nearby chair and deposited Victoria. She was still out of it, but Sands was encouraged to see one hand reach up to scratch her nose. Rashid got his attention and pointed out a basket on the snack bar just within arm's reach. Sands nodded. Rashid snatched up two apples, handed one to Sands. They devoured the fresh fruit unselfconsciously as the Drones looked on.

"I think we should put the big one in restraints."

Like two deck guns, Sands' eyes swiveled slowly toward a slight young man with a Southeast Asian accent.

"Did you just say that out loud?"

The hammer in the young man's hands, held upright like a cross before a vampire, wilted under Sands' gaze. Sands looked at the fellow next to him—an Indian kid, if Sands were to guess. He held a thin kitchen knife in one hand like a baton, shaking so badly he could have been conducting *Flight of the Bumblebee.*

"Put down the steak knife, sonny. All of you. Put the toys down now and nobody gets hurt."

A tall African kid in high-water pants that revealed mismatched socks spoke up. "We know who you are."

"Then you know I'm not kidding."

The blond buzz-cut stepped forward and thrust a crackling stun gun in Sands' face.

"I don't care how badass you are, I've got a stun gun!"

In a move shocking in its suddenness and speed, Sands disarmed the young man, sending him to the deck, where he clutched his arm and howled in pain.

Sands held up the weapon. "No, *I've* got a stun gun. You've got a fractured wrist." To add insult to literal injury, Sands hadn't even dropped his apple. He took one last bite and tossed the core aside.

Everyone dropped their weapons. The Indian kid raised his hands, and the others followed suit.

"Jesus, this ain't a western. Put your hands down and pick that shit up and put it away." Sands turned to Rashid and gestured toward the kid on the deck, still holding his arm. "Take care of him, Doc."

Rashid shook his head, disapproving of Sands' methods, but obeying his order. As he examined the kid's arm, the young woman opened a locker. "I'll get the first aid kit."

Everyone else picked up their "weapons" and put them back where they belonged. Sands noticed that Ahmer picked up the apple core from where Sands had tossed it and placed it in the waste bin. He told him, "Introduce me to your friends."

Ahmer did so. There was Bao, a spiky-haired go-getter from Shanghai with a brash smile. Desmond was the tall African, from Zambia, whose mismatched hand-me-downs clashed with his perfect, Oxford-accented English. Hari, from Mumbai, was a dyed-in-the-wool nerd whose play for cool points took the form of garish, high-top sneakers he wore in the "American style" with the laces undone. Then there was Ulani—"Lani for short"—a navy brat from Guam with a streak of magenta in her long, black hair.

"And that's Oleg," Ahmer finished, pointing at the big Slavic kid with the now-bandaged wrist, whose blond buzz-cut and leather combat boots gave off a definite skin-head vibe.

They were a colorful, proudly geeky lot. With better clothes they might have been the multinational ideal of some Silicon Valley megacorporation, the cream of the crop from the world's elite technical universities, reinventing the digital landscape between rounds of company-sanctioned ping-pong and proprietary-blend smoothies. But these kids would never see the inside of a digital startup, never get closer to a venture capitalist than stitching their designer clothes in some third-world sweatshop, like their less fortunate siblings or cousins. The Drones had avoided that fate through their intellect and technical skill, but their impoverished backgrounds left them easily exploitable, perfect candidates for the extra-legal prison-for-profit scheme represented by *Inferno*.

Sands asked no questions and showed no interest in the information each volunteered. If he wanted to know more—which he was pretty sure he didn't—he knew he would do better to talk to each of them individually. For now, knowing their names just made it easier to tell them what to do.

"I'm Sands," he said. "That's Rashid, and that's Victoria. So now we're all friends. What's the situation?"

-8-

All animals are equal, but some animals are more equal than others.

—George Orwell

"The evacuation begin this morning," Ahmer began, in his haphazard English. "First the Warden and staff. Then crew, then merc guards and Marines."

"So there's nobody else left?" Sands didn't want to leave any room for error.

"Just us. And the inmates."

"The Marines said they'd send the copter back for us," Bao added. "But Oleg overheard them laughing about it."

Sands turned to Oleg, who was sitting in one of the console chairs now, glumly nursing his wrist. "Is that right? You sure that's what they were laughing about?"

"Yeah," Oleg sneered. "They said we weren't worth the fuel to come back for us."

"Anyway, the laugh is on them," Bao said. "The shock-wave hit when they were taking off."

"Yeah, I saw the wreckage. Hilarious. So whatever's going on, they had a heads-up. Any ideas on that?"

Hari spoke up, his dark eyebrows knit in a severe line behind the black rims of his glasses. "We suspect it relates somehow to the situation in North Korea."

"No shit," Sands shot back. He indicated the blinking consoles of the work stations. "So you guys are running the ship?"

The Drones exchanged glances.

"No," Ahmer said.

"So who is?"

"We don't know."

Sands stared back at them, one eyebrow arched in question.

"The whole ship is run by computers," Bao explained. There was a tone of barely concealed geek condescension in his voice, but Sands let it slide. "We monitor everything from here. When orders come down from the Bridge, we execute them." He tapped some keys at a console. "But our controls are dead."

"But the ship's still running." Sands made his question sound like a statement.

"Sure," Lani put in. "It's like we're the brain. The brain's been cut off, but the nervous system is still functioning."

"But not like a chicken." Hari wanted to swallow his words the moment Sands looked at him, but he pushed on. "You know. With the head cut off. Not going in circles. The ship's on a course."

"So where are we going?"

Ahmer indicated a digital compass. "North. To the pole."

"We think the plan is to destroy the ship," Desmond said. In his cultured accent, he sounded authoritative beyond his years. "To wreck it on the ice."

Behind him, Sands heard Victoria mutter something, but he couldn't make it out. She had been moved to one of the cots, and Rashid sat at her side. She tossed her head, the unintelligible words tumbling out. Rashid patted her hand, and the muttering stopped. He looked at Sands and shrugged.

Sands turned back to Desmond. "Sounds shaky to me. These days, polar ice is scarce as hen's teeth." He gestured toward Hari. "To continue the chicken metaphor."

A snort from Oleg. He got to his feet, wincing as his wrist shifted position. "I heard something else. From the Marines. Something about 'setting the charge.' That's why they were laughing. Nothing's being left to chance."

"You mean—blow up the ship?" A note of panic was in Hari's voice.

"But—" Lani appealed to the others. "All these people."

Oleg looked at Lani with acid irony. "Dregs and Drones."

"Okay," Sands said, moving on from a belabored point. "So let's assume we've got a bomb, probably on a timer. Any idea where?"

Victoria was muttering again.

"Below decks," Oleg said.

"That doesn't exactly narrow it down."

"Sands!"

It was Rashid. Victoria had gone into some kind of frenzy, clawing at the back of her head like she meant to rip off her scalp. Her muttering had become a slurred moan, the same words again and again: "The chip—the chip—the chip—"

Rashid tried to restrain her, but Sands could see her fingertips were already bloodied.

"The chip—the chip—chip—chip—"

Lani, who was closest, grabbed one of Victoria's flailing arms by the wrist. Rashid had the other, but Victoria only slid from the cot and banged her head on the floor, her moaning growing to a shout.

At the sight of her thrashing on the floor, her arms flailing at Rashid and Lani, fear swept through the other Drones. They backed away, stumbling over each other.

"She's a Psych," Bao breathed. He picked up his hammer.

Sands grabbed the hammer and pushed Bao aside. "Let's not start that again." He swept Victoria up from the floor and put her in a bear hug, pinning her arms to her sides.

"Victoria! Victoria! Snap out of it!"

Unable to claw any more at her scalp, she whipped her head backwards, stunning Sands with a blow to the nose. His face was spackled with red, but it wasn't his blood.

"Jesus, Rashid, help me!"

Rashid held a hand over one eye. He'd taken a shot from one of Victoria's elbows. Lani had gone over the cot and was picking herself up from the deck. Rashid looked at Lani. "The medical kit. A sedative." Lani went for the kit, but Rashid expressed second thoughts. "But I don't know what drugs are already in her system. It could be dangerous."

"The chip—THE CHIP!"

Victoria whipped her head back again, but Sands dodged it. His instinct was to squeeze tighter, but the tighter he squeezed, the harder she fought. Instead, he eased the pressure, whispering into her ear. "Easy, Victoria, easy. It's Sands. I'm here..."

She ceased struggling, and her body went limp, the wild shouting lapsing into bare mumbling, then silence. Sands eased her back onto the cot. He knelt at her side and brushed her hair back from her face, his hand coming away with a smear of red.

"I'll dress her wound," Rashid said, kit in hand.

Sands washed the blood from his face and hands at a sink next to the snack bar. As he patted his face with a towel that looked like it had been too long from the laundry, Rashid called to him again.

"Sands!"

"Jesus, Rashid, what now?"

"There's something here. Under her scalp."

Sands came over and looked where Rashid had cleaned away the blood. He saw something dark under the skin. He thought it was just more blood at first, but Rashid dabbed at it with a cotton ball, and its outline became clear. It was geometric in shape.

"Get it out."

Rashid found a scalpel in the med kit, and with just the tip made a tiny incision. The Drones crowded around to see as Rashid probed the incision with tweezers.

"I've got it."

He withdrew the tweezers and held up what looked like a bloodied piece of plastic.

"What is it?" Sands asked.

His answer came in a barely audible whisper from Victoria. "The chip . . . ."

"Let me see." Oleg took it from Rashid, looked it over, held it for the others to see. They exchanged glances that conveyed more than Sands could follow. Lani took the chip from Oleg, gave it a thorough cleaning with alcohol and an aerosol duster, and plugged it into a console. Ahmer sat down and tapped a few keys. The monitor came alive with diagrams and data.

"What is it" Hari asked.

Sands looked at Ahmer's wide eyes as they scanned the screen. "Everything."

·9·

*The first problem for all of us, men and women, is not to
learn, but to unlearn.*

—Gloria Steinem

Ahmer, Hari, and Bao worked at their separate consoles, poring through the chip's data. As Ahmer had said,
it had everything—blueprints, specs, diagrams—all there
was to know about the design and function of the ship.
Oleg hovered over them, commenting on whatever appeared on their screens, directing them to check out this
or that file. Sands hung back, trying to get as much of a
sense of the data as he could, but letting Oleg have his
head. The young Slav saw himself as the group leader, and
after the way Sands had humiliated him, it didn't hurt to
let him have a little of his pride back.

Ahmer pointed at an image on his screen. "There's the
engine room." Oleg leaned over him, but Ahmer addressed Sands. "If we don't get control of the ship from
here, we could use the engine room controls."

"Can we access it?"

"Most definitely. The plans are uploaded to the system now. Wherever we are, we can access them from our handhelds, and they tell us where to go."

"Okay, let's say we get to the engine room. How do we know those controls haven't been over-ridden too, just like the ones up here? I mean, it's just more computers, right?"

"Find the rudder room," Oleg said. "It has manual controls. We can change course from there, if we have to."

"That's a good idea," Sands acknowledged. "But help me understand this. Your handhelds work, your monitors work, so why don't your ship controls work?"

It was another one of those moments in which the Drones all paused to look significantly at one another, as if there was some subconscious geek communication going on that Sands wasn't privy to.

"What?" Sands prompted.

Oleg smiled like someone who didn't think much of smiling. "It seems we have a ghost interface."

The ugly smirk made Sands want to break Oleg's other wrist. "English."

"A hidden access to the system," Ahmer translated. "I think maybe it is some other thing more than that. Maybe a parallel system. We still control part. But some other body controls the rest."

Off Sands' quizzical look, Hari further translated. "He means somebody else."

"Like a person? A person on the ship?"

"I think maybe so," Ahmer said.

With a wave of his hand—his non-fractured hand—Oleg dismissed Ahmer's suggestion. "Don't listen to him. Why would anybody stay behind just to steer the ship into an iceberg? It's on autopilot."

Sands had to admit Oleg's point made sense, but he didn't want to jump to any conclusions.

"So if there is this 'some other body,' where would he be? Any ideas on that?"

Ahmer consulted with Hari a moment, scrolled through some files, and pulled up a diagram that was an array of lines converging from all different directions. "This is something strange we noticed. Too much circuitry for no purpose. The ghost interface could be from there. But I don't think we want to go."

"Why not?"

That smile from Oleg again. "That's the Psycho Ward."

"Remember how it was in the old days?" a voice intoned from out of nowhere. "Before Tastes Like Mom's?" Everyone looked up at the overhead video monitors, the same as the ones in the prisoners' cells. They had popped to life, right on schedule.

"Oh, this is a good one," Lani said, with no hint of irony.

Sands looked on in dumb amazement as the Drones watched a black-and-white image from an old television show with the same rapt attention as any Dreg in a cell block. The show was from well before Sands' time, but he recognized the clip from an episode of *I Love Lucy*, the one in which Lucy is trying to do a commercial for a horrible-tasting health food called Vitameatavegamin.

"Jesus, can't we shut those things off?"

Sands' question was answered by a round of laughter from the Drones as Lucy gagged on the foul-tasting concoction. "It's so tasty, too!"

"Hey, look at this." Bao had on his screen what looked like a dossier for an inmate, complete with mugshot. He pulled up another and another, scrolling through them like a slideshow.

"Must be the ship's manifest," Oleg said.

Sands and the Drones all crowded around, fascinated by the stream of faces: all ages, all races, all nationalities, from the poor and vagrant, whose empty eyes bespoke a life on the margins, to those whose defiant gazes and careful grooming told of a privileged life that must have once seemed untouchable. They were all the "before" pictures, the last images of the persons who had become *Inferno's* faceless disappeared.

"Don't you boys know it's impolite to look through a girl's things?"

They all turned to see Victoria, unsteady, but on her feet, a weak smile directed at Sands.

"Hi, soldier."

Inspired by the *I Love Lucy* clip, Sands affected his best Ricky Ricardo voice: "Lucy, you got some 'splaining to do."

Victoria didn't have a comeback. She wobbled on her feet, as if the ground beneath her had suddenly pitched. Sands caught her and eased her back to the cot.

"Do you know where you are?"

"Yeah. It's a little fuzzy. One of the prison ships."

"*Inferno*," Sands told her. She nodded vaguely, recalling a forgotten name.

"Hey," Bao called from his console. He had continued to scroll through the prisoner manifest. "I recognize some of these people."

Everyone gathered around as he read the name under one of the mugshots: "'Rabbi Sholem Ben-Ezra.' He won the Nobel Peace Prize!"

Sands stared at the image in disbelief: A mild-looking man with soulful blue eyes, a kind smile, and a freckled, clean-shaven dome balanced by a thick, salt-and-pepper beard.

"Bloodyface."

He whispered the name as if invoking some forbidden, profane entity. A wave of disbelief, immediately replaced by shocked recognition, rippled through everyone there.

"How could that be?" Ahmer asked.

Victoria, still too weak to stand on her feet, explained: "*Inferno* specializes in political prisoners—dissidents, opposition leaders..." She looked at Sands. "Trouble-makers."

Sands forced a smile, but he couldn't take his eyes off the image of "Bloodyface" from a very different life. Rabbi Ben-Ezra had been a world hero for leading a grassroots reconciliation movement between the Israelis and Palestinians, but hardline government and religious leaders denounced him as a traitor. Sands remembered something about a sex scandal. Most people seemed to believe the charges were trumped up, but there had been an arrest and a trial. Sands couldn't remember more than that, but it all had a familiar ring that left a sick feeling in his stomach.

"But," Ahmer persisted, "how did a man of such peace become the Bloodyface?"

No one had an answer for that.

Bao moved on, and Sands and the others watched as more mugshots flashed across the screen, wondering who they all had been before *Inferno*, and how many of them were the faces of innocent people.

"So they're all political prisoners?" Lani asked.

"Not all," Victoria said. "Enough."

"Whoa, whoa," Sands interrupted. A face had caught his eye. "Go back."

Bao backtracked through the images until Sands told him to stop. Bao read off the name: "'Ray Leflore.' You know him?"

"I know him," Sands said. He gave no indication whether the beefy man with the thousand-yard stare was an old friend or enemy, but Bao thought from the way Sands stared at the image that the man must have some great importance.

Sands grabbed a pencil and paper, scribbled some names, and handed the list to Bao. "Here. Check these names."

"On it."

"Mr. Sands," Hari called. "I think I found something you want."

Sands went to Hari's console. At first, it just looked like more undecipherable schematics, but Hari pointed to a rectangular space labeled "Magazine."

"Doesn't this word mean..."

Sands clapped a meaty paw on Hari's thin shoulder and smiled.

"Weapons."

Just saying the word conjured for Sands the smell of gun oil and cordite. He took a moment to assess his crew. Victoria was still too weak to exert herself. Rashid was fit enough, considering his age and years of imprisonment, but Sands needed a wise head in the Vestibule. He almost regretted now breaking Oleg's wrist. At least he had some fighting spirit. The rest of the Drones struck Sands as a hopelessly nerdy and action-averse bunch. He needed three men—but he'd make do with what he had.

"Ahmer, Bao, Desmond—you three come with me."

"Where are we going?" Ahmer asked.

Sands pointed at the screen. "Hari found a cache of weapons. We're gonna go get 'em...before somebody else does."

Sands saw out of the corner of his eye that Hari was hurt at not being included in the party. He didn't really care, but good team leadership meant keeping everybody in the game and feeling positive.

"Good job, Hari." He grabbed from Bao's station the list of names he had written up and handed it to Hari. "Here's a list of names I want you to check against the prisoner manifest. Top priority, okay?"

"Okay, Mr. Sands."

"The rest of you, sit tight till we get back. If you want something to do, keep combing through that data for anything that looks interesting." He turned to his excursion team. "All right, fellas, grab your butter knives and sharpened pencils. Let's go."

"I want to go, too!" Lani piped up, her tuft of magenta hair bobbing with enthusiasm.

"No girls," Sands said, biting his tongue too late as he watched Lani's brimming smile collapse into a girlish pout. So much for team leadership. Oh, well, there was a reason Sands had never advanced to command.

Sands turned away, his guard down, totally unprepared for the crouching spin move that took his feet out from under him. Before he knew what was happening he was on his back, Lani astride his chest with a perfectly aimed kung fu chop suspended an inch from his throat.

"Okay," he said. "Girls."

-10-

There is no education like adversity.
—Benjamin Disraeli

"Whoa, look at all this firepower!"

When Sands unsealed the hatch to the weapons cache, his youthful entourage rushed in like kids at a toy store. He didn't bother trying to hold them back because he saw immediately that the racks of weapons were all safely locked up. Nobody was going to pull a gun from the wall and shoot their foot off, at least. The room was smaller than he had expected, and despite Bao's enthusiastic assessment, he found the "firepower" anemic. There were shotguns, handguns, tactical grenades, and a variety of batons and ballistic armor—the usual riot control stuff. It was enough, maybe, to put down a medium-size prison riot, but if the sixty thousand inmates of *Inferno* ever really cut loose, shotguns and tear gas would be like a flyswatter against a grizzly bear.

The ship's plans called the room a "magazine," which implied explosive armament. But Sands saw nothing in the compartment more explosive than a flash-bang. In size, the cache didn't qualify as a magazine, or an armory—it was really no more than a weapons locker. And why wasn't it located above decks instead of below? In an emergency, the number one thing you want in a weapon is accessibility. Were the designers of *Inferno* really that confident that the inmates posed no threat to control of the ship? Or could it have been that the guards and crew were ultimately just as expendable as the inmates? If it was true, as Oleg and the other Drones believed, that the ship was being scuttled with ninety-nine percent of its total population still aboard, what guarantee was there for that other one percent, if the corporate cost/benefit scale were to tip a few grains in the wrong direction?

Lani broke in on Sands' thoughts. "Hey, anybody have a key to unlock these guns?"

Sands turned to Ahmer. "Won't your sonic screwdriver, or whatever you call it, do that?"

Lani pulled on the cable that was looped through the trigger guards of the row of shotguns. It was secured by a conventional padlock.

"Wow," Bao said. "That's really old school."

Sands looked it over—hardened steel shank, laminated body, keyed locking mechanism. It was a padlock, all right. He remembered something G.K. used to say whenever the team was confronted in the field by some unexpectedly sophisticated technology: "Nothing outsmarts a computer like a good old-fashioned rock."

"We have bolt cutters in our tool kit in the Vestibule," Desmond offered.

"Yeah, that should work."

Desmond wondered if that was Sands' way of telling him to go top-deck and get the cutters. Or maybe he was being sarcastic. It was hard to tell with this guy. But after a moment it was clear that Sands' mind was on something else. He paced up and down the racks of gear, then from the hatch to the wall, trying to get a measure of the space.

"Something's not right," he said. "Ahmer, pull up those plans again."

Ahmer scrolled through the images on his tablet until he found the layout of the compartment. It was just a blank rectangle with a hatch indicated on the outer bulkhead. The rectangle was long and narrow, just like the compartment itself.

"Dimensions look okay," Ahmer said. "But look— what's this?"

He pointed out another blank rectangle, much bigger, that lay behind the back wall.

"I don't know much about blueprints," Sands said, "but they usually don't have big empty spaces like that, do they?"

"No. They don't."

"All right, everybody check that back wall. We're looking for a crack, a seam, maybe some kind of catch."

They all inspected different parts of the bulkhead, running their hands over surfaces, feeling behind racks of weapons and armor, but nobody could find anything.

"Hey, check out this fire alarm," Bao said. He pointed at a glass-covered, red rectangle mounted on the wall opposite from where they had been searching. "I don't think it's a fire alarm."

"I think you're right," Sands said. The box didn't have any markings referring to fire or an alarm. Behind the square of glass was nothing but a round red button, like a panic button. The cover that framed the glass window was locked with a small brass padlock that could easily have been jimmied with a screwdriver. But Sands figured there was a reason the cover was made of glass. He knocked it out with a tap from his elbow.

"All right, everybody stand clear of that back wall." He punched the button, and a series of explosive bolts cut a neat rectangle in the bulkhead, revealing a large metal door, like that of a bank vault.

"I think we just found our magazine." Sands inspected the hand-wheel on the door, tested the latch handle. Both were fixed tight. "No padlock on this one. Think you can open it, Ahmer?"

Ahmer stepped up, massaged the keypad of his handheld with a motion somewhere between playing a piano and milking a cow. Several times he looked expectantly at the latch, only to go back to the keypad.

"Des, it looks like we might need those bolt cutters after all."

Missing the irony, Desmond took a stutter-step toward the hatch before he either caught himself or was stopped by the ping of the electronic lock.

"Got it!"

Sands acknowledged Ahmer's grin with a nod and spun the wheel-lock. With a pneumatic hiss, the six-inch-thick door swung open.

"Holy shit," someone said. It was the consensus view.

Even Sands was taken aback by the weapons bonanza. The automatic rifles, high-caliber machine guns, and grenade launchers weren't really a surprise. But why would the guards of a prison ship ever need surface-to-air missiles? And it wasn't just the type of weapons that surprised him, it was the quantity. There were tons of them, enough to outfit an army. Including handguns, Sands thought there were probably enough to arm every person on the ship—guards, Drones, and inmates alike.

"Why so many weapons?" Desmond wanted to know.

"And why hide them like this?" Lani wondered. "Like they're super top secret."

"Two good questions," Sands said.

"Maybe Miss Brzinski have the answers," Ahmer offered.

"I wouldn't be surprised." Sands took a wicked-looking bullpup from one of the racks, hefted it appreciatively, and cracked open a box of ammo. "Okay, folks, time for a crash course in military armaments and self-defense."

***

It was a delicate matter arming the Drones. Lani claimed to know her way around an AR—at least she said she could load one and shoot it "without killing anybody."

"Well," Sands retorted, "the idea might be to kill *somebody.*"

Lani replied that he knew what she meant, which he did, but he couldn't resist needling her. She was a little put off by the backwards configuration of the bullpup, which she held in her hands like an unwanted gift. "Why is the magazine behind the trigger?"

"Don't worry about it. You load one and you pull the other. The fact that you know the difference tells me you'll be okay."

She smiled at that. Sands didn't smile back, but he happened to notice that Ahmer did. It only lasted an instant before teenage awkwardness prevailed and the two guilty parties suddenly became fascinated by their shoes. But it occurred to Sands that he had caught Ahmer several times looking at Lani the way hopelessly hormonal nerds have been looking at attractive young women since the days of slide rules and T-squares. Sands filed this observation in his growing store of Headaches I Don't Need.

Sands decided the best course of action was for each of the Drones to carry an unloaded rifle strapped over each shoulder and a backpack full of charged magazines. To his own back he strapped a grenade launcher and a shotgun. Altogether, it made for a hefty load, but better to get what they could carry now rather than take a chance on being left short if they couldn't get back to the cache. In case of direst emergency, Sands instructed them on how to load and fire their weapons, but he made it clear no one was to touch their rifles unless either he ordered them to or he was dead. "And even if I'm dead, you better think twice."

He also outfitted each of them with a knife, tear gas grenades, and a baton, which he instructed them to carry in their hands at all times. If they did come under attack, they would at least have their batons at the ready, and the worst damage they could do to themselves would be to drop them on their toes.

Once everyone was outfitted, they resealed the vault and closed the hatch. Sands didn't like leaving the riot gear so poorly secured, but he figured they would be back soon enough. Luckily, he aired his concerns—just in the habitual way he had picked up over years of running operations with many moving parts—because Ahmer and his magic keypad had a solution.

"Every hatch has a mechanical latch and an electronic latch," he explained. He touched a few keys, and the latch clicked, a tiny LED indicator going from red to green. "Now, no one can open it unless they are hooked into the main system."

"Okay," Sands said with a nod. He would have to remember to stop taking this kid for granted. He had knowledge and technical knowhow Sands lacked. "Can you get Hari on that thing?"

"Sure," Ahmer said. "It has a function similar to cell phone."

He touched a few keys, the device crackled, and Hari's voice said, "Ahmer?"

Ahmer looked at Sands. "Go ahead. You're on speaker."

"Hari, this is Sands. Do you have those names I gave you?"

"I found two, Mr. Sands."

"That's good. Can you send the information to Ahmer for me?"

"It's on the way."

Sands hefted his bullpup in the ready position. "All right, everybody. Saddle up."

"Where are we going?" Lani wanted to know.

"Deck Eight."

"Deck Eight? Why?"

"Reinforcements."

-11-

A religion that a person has not made for himself is a superstition and not a religion.

—Martin Luther

Ray Leflore sat on his bunk, staring, as he often did, at the legend emblazoned on the bulkhead across from his cell: **8 FRAUD 8**.

When he had first come to *Inferno*, three years ago now, the word had made him angry. Anger was the "sin" designated for Deck Five, and he would have felt much more at home there. Or they could have placed him on Gluttony Deck. It would have been an insult, but at least it would have made some kind of sense, considering how he liked to pack it in. Violence Deck would have been more appropriate, since that was how he had lived his life. He could even have accepted Heresy Deck, because, in a way, he had long ago thrown over everything he once believed in. But how was he a *fraud*?

He had told himself the word was meaningless, just an in-joke of some architect who had a fancy for Dante, and it had nothing to do with a prisoner's crimes, real or fabricated. Or, even if the deck names were intended as meaningful labels, the reality was that prisons got crowded and inmates were placed wherever there was space. Ray had been a late-comer to the ship, helicoptered in long after it had filled most of its cells and put out to sea. But every day, there was the word, in giant block letters, staring him right in the face, the first thing he saw in the morning and the last thing he saw at night. After a while, such things work on a man.

Ray had never been the contemplative type, but that word had turned him practically into a Buddhic navel-gazer. He considered all the ways he had been a fraud in his life—his failures as a husband and father, his carefully cultivated tough-guy aura, his need to make jokes in the face of death, his dedication to defending a nation that had never been kind to him or others of his race. The self-inquiry had started almost as a game, and he was surprised how easily he came up with convincing evidence of his fraudulent nature. Before long, the obvious instances were exhausted. The game became a challenge, and as he delved deeper, a habit. And a habit in prison is a way of life. Fraud, he realized, was the very essence of *Inferno* and everything it contained, from the phony "justice" it meted out to its prisoners to the phony "Process" it doled out as food. As a young man still in thrall to the daily Bible lessons conducted by his pious father, Ray's favorite scripture had been Ecclesiastes, with its famous verse: "Vanity of vanities! All is vanity!" Here, in his tiny wire cage in the belly of *Inferno*, he had devised his own scripture: "Fraud of frauds! All is fraudulent!" It didn't have quite the same poetic ring, but it had the virtue of being true. And once he had seized on that bit of wisdom, he made peace with his verbal tormentor. If he was a fraud, it was because he was of a fraudulent world.

So he sat on his bunk. Staring at that word but thinking about other things: about the lights that still dimly burned, about the video feeds that still followed their familiar schedule, about the Process that still extruded onto his waiting tray at the appointed times. The ship's clockwork mechanism was still purring along, but what did it really signify? It was all calculated to make him think that things were normal, that someone who knew what he was doing was in control, that all was well.

But all was not well. An explosion had rocked the ship. The power had been interrupted. There had been chaos above decks, and now a dead quiet. He had heard the rumors that the crew had abandoned ship, that some stray Drone was wandering below decks, freeing prisoners according to some plan only he knew. He had even heard one of the freed prisoners was a woman.

Ray knew better than to believe ship's rumors, but he also knew better than to dismiss them. His cell was close to the main elevator, and he had heard the familiar whine of its machinery several times since morning. After years of listening to it, he could tell if the car was going up or down, and even at which deck it was stopping. Someone had descended to Deck Nine that morning, then back to Top-deck. Then down to Deck Three. Since then, the elevator had been silent, neither descending to the lower decks, nor returning home to the top. But Ray had the sense that someone was still moving through the ship.

He was too far from the service stairs to hear any movement there himself, but someone had heard or seen something, and word was spreading like slow, rumbling thunder. Someone was coming.

***

The elevator had been okay for the short trip down to the magazine on Deck Three, but Sands wanted to be more discreet in reaching Fraud Deck, the last deck before the ship's deepest pit, and his old home, Treachery. It was slower going down the stairs of the service shaft, but the walls were solid and Sands and his crew were shielded from prying eyes. Someone may hear their footfalls on the metal steps, but if seeing was believing, hearing was only a rumor, and Sands felt the less his fellow inmates knew about who he was and what he was doing, the better.

Still, it was remarkable how the murmurings of the rumor mill so closely tracked their movements. When they arrived at the landing designated **8 FRAUD 8**, it was as if the whole cell block had been waiting for them. Sands immediately regretted bringing Lani along, because her presence on the mezzanine set off a cacophony of jeering and cat-calling that rattled his skull. The Drones cowered back in the stair well, but when Sands forged ahead they quickly followed, Lani scuttling up to him so close he almost tripped over her. She was crowding his gun hand, but Sands said nothing. She was understandably scared, and it wasn't lost on him that some of the sex-starved crazies on the block were already jerking off in their cells. There was nothing to do but keep moving—get what they came for and get out.

"Which cell?"

Ahmer consulted his hand-held. "Opposite end. By the elevator."

"Of course. Glad we didn't come that way."

"But you said—"

"Keep moving."

By the time they got to the end of the mezzanine, inmates were throwing things—Sands didn't want to know what. Fortunately, the cell was situated where the mezzanine joined the central shaft structure, and it was shielded somewhat from the view of the other inmates and their projectiles.

Sands stopped, the Drones crowding behind him like chicks behind a mother hen. The man he saw sitting in the cell before him was thinner than the last time he had seen him, with maybe a little gray at the temples, an extra line in his brow. But for the strange expression on his face, Sands would have known him anywhere. Ray LeFlore looked at Sands with penetrating eyes, as if he recognized this ghost from the past but meant to stare him down until he proved his reality or dissolved into mist.

As the two men continued to stare at one another the Drones became antsy, but at last the man in the cell spoke.

"Sands."

"Catfish."

For a moment, Sands thought his old friend might burst into tears, and he could not have stood that. Sands warded off any rising sentiment with a crooked smile. "So, you ready to stop sitting on your sorry ass and start kicking some?"

Catfish smiled. He rose from his bunk and came to the grate. "Laissez les bon temps roulez."

Desmond leaned over to Bao and whispered, "This is weird."

In a moment, Ahmer had sprung the hatch and Catfish was out of his cell. The two old friends approached each other awkwardly.

"For a second there I wasn't sure you were real. Then I wasn't sure if you'd come to bust me out or kill me."

"Kill you? Shit, Catfish—"

"Don't act like you don't know what I'm talking about."

Sands knew. He'd had plenty of long nights when he thought he could have easily killed any one of his old compatriots for their apparent betrayal at his trial. But now...

"That was a long time ago, Cat."

Catfish nodded. "They drugged us."

"I knew that."

He didn't. But now it all made sense.

"If you guys are gonna hug it out, I wish you'd get it over with so we can get out of here."

Catfish looked at Lani with a quizzical eye. "So she's real, too? I thought sure *that* was my imagination."

Lani cocked her head. "Ha. Ha."

Sands and Catfish embraced, thumping each other on the back.

"Glad to see you, Bro."

"Glad to be seen."

"All right," Lani pleaded. "Let's go!"

"One second." Sands took one of Ahmer's rifles and a loaded magazine and held them to Catfish. His old friend eyed the weapon appreciatively.

"Whatcha got there, an XM, full auto?"

"Only the best for you, Bro."

"Nice!" He took the bullpup, rammed the magazine home, and threw the bolt.

"How come he gets a loaded one?" Bao demanded.

"How many people you killed with one of these?" Catfish asked him. Bao was silent. "That's why."

"All right." Sands turned to Ahmer. "Point the way."

Following his tablet like a divining rod, Ahmer led the party through several twists and turns to another block on the same level. There they found Angel, doing pull-ups from a pipe that ran across the ceiling of his cell. At the sight of Sands and his party Angel froze in mid-air, let out a whoop, and did a somersault, sticking the landing like a gymnast. Unlike Sands and Catfish, Angel was untroubled by doubt or recriminations about the past, and he regarded his old friends with a broad grin.

"Shit, it's about time you two gold-brickers came and got me. Where you been?"

"Up on Lust Deck bangin' yo' mamma."

Bao and Desmond looked at one another with wide eyes. "D-a-a-a-m-n!"

The Drones may have been taken aback by Catfish's salty comeback, but Angel's grin never wavered. Ahmer opened the hatch, and Angel came out and greeted everyone in the party with the half-handshake, half-hug combo he'd picked up as a kid on the streets of East L.A.

"I knew you were coming, Sands. I saw it like a vision in my dreams. I watched you in the Arena, Bro, and I said to myself, one of these days Sands is gonna bust outta this shithole, and I'm gonna bust with him. It's destiny, man, I'm telling you. I didn't know you was here, Catfish, but I'm glad to see you. How you doing?"

Angel talked a mile a minute, like he wanted to catch up on the last three years right on the spot. Sands shut him up momentarily by unstrapping one of Lani's bullpups and handing it to him.

"You still know how to use one of these?"

Angel caressed the weapon like a pet cat. "Like a fish knows how to swim, Bro."

"We've got another man to pick up."

"Who's that, Sands?"

"Wolf."

"That's cool. Any others?"

"Don't know yet. We're still looking. Ahmer, you got him pinpointed?"

"Yes, but we have to take the elevator again. He's not on this level."

"Okay." With a whistle, Sands directed his troupe back from where they had come. They double-timed it past the gantlet of cat-calling prisoners, but they had no trouble as they crossed the mezzanine and made it back to the elevator.

After all were boarded, Sands asked, "Which deck?"

Ahmer swallowed before he answered. "Seven."

"Are you sure?"

Ahmer nodded.

"That's the Psycho Ward." Angel crossed himself.

"So what?" Sands said. "They're all locked up in cages, just like everybody else."

"Yeah," Bao put in, "but they're batshit crazy."

"Maybe not all," Desmond offered. "The Psycho Ward doesn't take up the whole deck."

"They call it Violence Deck for a reason, Desmond." Bao stabbed the air with an imaginary dagger. "They're all violent psychotics!"

Catfish tugged at Sands' sleeve. "You sure about this, Sands? If Wolf's in the Psycho Ward..." He tapped his temple. "He's probably gone."

"Well, then, we need to find out, don't we?" Sands punched the button and the elevator jolted into motion.

-12-

Whoever fights monsters should see to it that in the pro-cess he does not become one.

—Friedrich Nietzsche

Once the elevator grumbled to a stop and the doors split, the legend **7 VIOLENCE 7** stared back at Sands and his party like a threat. Unlike Deck Eight, here there were no reverberations of the rumor mill, no catcalls from inmates, and the backup lights that ran on emergency power were even fewer and dimmer. There wasn't quite silence—movement could be heard in the darkened cells, and voices muttered and hissed in streams of incoherent syllables. As Sands stepped out onto the deck a single, piercing wail echoed from someplace in the far shadows. It froze the party in their tracks.

"I think that was Psych talk for 'welcome aboard,'" Catfish quipped.

Sands took a reluctant Ahmer by the elbow and pulled him forward. "Which way?"

Ahmer pointed down a corridor illuminated by flickering lights. Seeing the fear on the faces of the four young Drones, Sands led the way. "Say when."

The cells lining either side of the corridor were mostly dark, but the living shapes within them were evident. Many were prostrate and still in their bunks, one even lying on the deck, unconscious or dead. Some stood and brooded from the shadows, some gripped the grates with claw-like hands, and still others paced back and forth like caged panthers. A few called out as the party passed, bleating like animals, whistling, or shouting. One, in a clear, articulate voice calmly stated, "I want to eat your face."

Most of the inmates looked human enough, but their faces were animalistic, some staring with predatory intensity, others rolling their eyes insanely.

"Eyes front!" Sands barked, sensing the waning resolve of his crew.

They came to an intersection, and Sands paused. "Which way?"

"Straight ahead," Ahmer replied.

The corridors right and left were brightly lit. Straight ahead was a long tunnel of darkness with an ominous glow at the end.

"Figures." Sands trudged on.

The cells along this corridor appeared to be empty, and in the silence, the only sound was the clatter of their footsteps on the deck. The light at the end of the corridor defined itself as a rectangle, and as they got closer, the outline of a cell. Sands could make out the monitor hanging from the ceiling, the toilet and sink, and the bunk along the back wall. Lying on the bunk was the shape of a man. Wolf.

"That's it," Ahmer whispered.

As they neared, Wolf didn't move. He lay on his back, eyes, closed, his hands folded across his chest, almost like a corpse laid out for burial.

Self-conscious of the sound of their footfalls in the silence, the group walked softly, but the metal deck resounded with an unmistakable clatter. Wolf must have heard them approach, but he didn't stir. Sands stopped and raised a fist. The Drones came to a halt, a safe three or four paces back. Catfish and Angel joined Sands, and—to Sands' surprise—Ahmer stepped forward with them.

They looked down at the man in the cell, perfectly still, except for the rise and fall of his chest. He looked much like the Wolf of old—paler, but lean and muscled, with a thick brush of prematurely silver hair that he had somehow managed to keep close-cropped, if ragged. Angel looked at Catfish. Catfish looked at Sands. Sands shrugged. Why didn't he move? Maybe Catfish had been right, that Wolf was "gone."

But then Wolf opened his eyes, slowly turned his head, and stared at the men staring back at him. He smiled.

Ahmer lifted his hand-held in a silent gesture to ask if he should spring the latch, but Sands stayed him.

"Wolf, we're all glad to see you looking so cheerful, but you're in the Psycho Ward, man. You're going to have to say something if you want us to let you out."

Wolf swung his feet to the deck and sat up with a sigh. "Aw, you know I was never the chatty type."

With no more than that, Sands told Ahmer to open the hatch. Wolf stepped through, and Sands put a hand on his shoulder.

"Are you okay, Wolf? I mean, really okay?"

"They put something in the food. It does something to you." He indicated the row of empty cells. "I've seen it. All these men...I'm okay now, but if they'd kept me here much longer..." He shook his head. Sands embraced him, slapped him hard on the back. Angel and Catfish took their turns doing the same.

Without being told or asking permission, Wolf relieved Desmond of one of his two rifles, slammed a magazine home, and stuffed two more in his belt.

"Hail, hail, the gang's all here," Catfish said.

"Not all," Sands replied. "Not G.K."

***

Feeling woozy from watching too long as Hari scrolled through hundreds of mugshots and profiles, Victoria plopped down at one of the unmanned consoles. She rubbed her eyes, which still felt raw and crusty, the backs of her eyelids like sandpaper. She asked Rashid if he had any eye drops in his kit. He brought it over and fished around, but stopped when movement on the surveillance video caught his attention. Victoria saw it, too.

"What is it?" Oleg had noticed them staring at the screens.

"Trouble."

On the video feed they could see inmates in one of the blocks pouring out of their cells. Oleg spat a Slavic curse and tapped his headset.

"Ahmer! Ahmer, do you read me?"

Ahmer's voice came over the speaker. "Here."

"There's been a breach. Prisoners out of their cells. What deck are you on?"

"Seven."

Oleg checked the monitor—it indicated Deck Seven.

"Shit! You've gotta get out of there."

Ahmer tapped into the video feed on his hand-held to bring up the images Oleg was seeing. As he gaped at the sight on his screen of perhaps a dozen inmates out of their cells, he bumped into Sands, who had come to an abrupt stop.

"Sands!"

Sands held up a hand. "I see them."

They were straight ahead, milling about, but giving no sign that they had noticed Sands or his party.

Ahmer hissed in Sands' ear. "We can go back and circle around to the elevator the other way."

Sands nodded and signaled a retreat. They all turned quietly, and after a half dozen careful strides it seemed they would escape without incident. But a whoop went up from one of the darkened cells they passed, and the Psychs came running.

"Go! Go! Go!" Wolf led from the rear, pumping his finger forward. No one hesitated, the whole party running full out, back from where they had come.

"Which way?" They were approaching the point where the dark and light corridors crossed. Sands saw that Ahmer was struggling to hold his joggling hand-held steady as he ran as fast as he could.

"Left!" It sounded like a guess.

They veered left, Wolf lagging behind just long enough to squeeze off a burst from his bullpup to discourage their pursuers. Sands caught a glimpse of Wolf pausing to see if the burst had had an effect, saw his look of disbelief as he goosed the bullpup again and ran for his life.

The steady light of the corridor washed over them like a calming bath, and Sands sensed the panic that had propelled them from the dark ebbing away. But unlike the other corridor, this one was fully populated by Psychs, and the sight of the party running in fear agitated them to a frenzy of shouts, growls, and unnerving laughter.

"Keep running," Sands shouted. "Don't slow down!" But Sands almost stopped dead when he heard a warning buzzer, and the row of LED indicators on the cells ahead suddenly flashed from green to red.

"Oh, no." The words formed in his head like a thought balloon in a comic book. Most of the Psychs hadn't realized what had happened yet, but one tested his hatch, and it fell open with a clank.

"Run!" Sands' legs were already burning, but he took off as if he meant to leave the others behind. He met the first Psychs out of their cages like a fullback at the scrimmage line, and they went down. He meant to clear a path, but in seconds the Psychs were streaming out of their cells, forming a gantlet of screaming, flailing bodies.

"Keep going," he shouted to the Drones. "We've got to make the elevator."

Sands, Wolf, and Catfish took on the Psychs with a fury, beating them down with batons, cracking their heads with the butt-ends of their bullpups, only firing a shot when they had to. They managed to get the Drones to the end of the corridor, but there were just too many Psychs coming from all directions. One had grabbed Lani from behind, but she managed to crush his instep with a well-placed kick and gouge his eye. His howl proved that even the Psychs felt pain.

Bao and Desmond were double-teaming another Psych, beating him down to the deck with their batons.

But Ahmer wasn't so lucky. A Psych had hold of his bull-pup and was trying to get leverage against Ahmer's flailing arms to crush his windpipe.

"If they get weapons we're in trouble," Catfish shouted, cracking another Psych across the face with his bullpup.

Sands ordered Angel and Wolf ahead to secure the elevator. "We'll catch up."

Sands took out Ahmer's assailant with a shot through the ear. The Psych crumpled, Ahmer's wide eyes gaping at the spray of blood. Catfish raked the corridor with a burst from his bullpup, sending the other Psychs diving back into their cells. Ahmer had collapsed into a lotus position, his bullpup in his lap. Sands helped him to his feet.

"You're okay, son." It was an order.

Bao and Desmond were still pummeling their foe, although he had long since stopped fighting, or possibly breathing.

"Guys. Guys! I think you got him."

Panting with effort, the two Drones stopped swinging their batons. They looked at Sands as if coming out of a dream.

Catfish sent another burst of machine gun fire raking across the bulkhead. "Let's go!"

Sands stood at the end of the corridor, urging the others through. It wasn't long before the Psychs were coming out of their cells, but once everyone in his team was safely through the hatch, Sands slammed it shut and jammed it with a baton.

They passed several dead bodies along the catwalk that led back to the mezzanine, where Angel and Wolf were waiting. Angel stood guard, nervously gripping his rifle as Wolf battered the elevator button with the side of his fist.

"It won't open!"

Sands looked to Ahmer. Somehow, Ahmer had managed to hold on to his device, but his hands shook so that he was having trouble operating it.

Banging at the end of the catwalk. Somehow the Psychs had pried the hatch open, and several hands groped through the gap trying to get hold of the baton and unjam it. If these really were Psychs, Sands thought, they weren't the mindless monsters everyone thought they were.

"Come on, Ahmer, you can do it."

Ahmer fixed his eyes on the hand-held with furious concentration, but his hands trembled so that he couldn't work the keypad. Bao looked at Sands, and quietly took the device from Ahmer. He worked the keys. The indicator beeped and flashed, but the elevator doors stayed shut.

"It's no good. Somebody's shut it down."

At the end of the catwalk, the baton clattered to the deck and the hatch swung open. Psychs began shoving through, slowed only by the numbers trying to crowd each other out.

Sands looked at Catfish. "Hand me that launcher."

He turned his back to Catfish, showing the grenade launcher he had secured by a strap. Catfish unfastened it and handed it over. Sands retrieved a grenade from his pack of ammunition, loaded, and aimed.

"Grab onto something."

Seeing the weapon, some of the Psychs tried to scramble back through the hatch, but there were too many trying to push through from the other side. Sands let the grenade fly. A ball of fire shook the ship down to its frame and unhinged the catwalk from its moorings. Somehow, the Psychs had managed to get the hatch closed, protecting most of them from the blast, but a half dozen on the catwalk went flying to their deaths.

The mezzanine sagged beneath Sands' feet. He slid down the sloping grate to the rail, but he managed to hang on. When he'd regained his footing, he turned to find his crew cowering and clinging to the mezzanine rails, all regarding him with looks of mixed amazement and relief.

Catfish said something, but Sands couldn't hear it for the ringing in his ears. He slung the launcher over his shoulder and nodded to the next nearest exit. "Looks like we're taking the stairs."

After the adrenaline stopped pumping, the climb to Top-deck was a strain on rubbery legs. Angel and Wolf were the least affected, and Angel even showed off for a huffing and puffing Catfish by turning around and taking the steps backwards.

"What's the matter, Cat? You getting old?"

Catfish smiled with good humor. "Too much high livin'."

Sands noticed Ahmer lagging behind, a hangdog look on his face.

"You okay?"

Ahmer looked at Sands with pain in his eyes. "I'm a coward. Not brave. Not like you."

Sands smiled and clapped him on the shoulder. "No, Ahmer, you're not like me. You're still human."

-13-

Any excuse will serve a tyrant.

—Aesop

Sands burst into the Vestibule, followed by Catfish and the others. Oleg and Victoria were standing over Hari, who continued to scroll through the prisoner manifest. Sands' eyes fixed on Oleg. He grabbed him and shoved him against the wall.

"How did those Dregs get loose?"

"I don't know!"

"Somebody had to open those cages!" Sands pressed his forearm against Oleg's throat. "Talk!"

"It wasn't me!" Oleg could barely get the words out. "I tried to warn you!"

Rashid extended a calming hand to Sands, but he knew better than to touch him in this state. "It's true, Sands. Oleg is not your enemy."

Sands glanced from Rashid to Victoria. He could see in both their faces they thought he was wrong. He relaxed his grip, but kept Oleg pinned.

"Convince me."

Angel and Wolf loomed behind him, glaring at Oleg with menace. Catfish was there, too, but something else had caught his eye. He pointed to the basket of fruit at the snack bar. "Is that...food?"

"It sure is. Help yourself."

The three men pounced on the bounty like starving hyenas. Sands couldn't help but smile at their childlike joy, but he quickly switched back to his war face before Oleg got the wrong idea.

"So?"

Oleg pointed to his work station, where the monitors were filled with ship's diagrams. "It's the Psycho Ward."

Sands let him go. "Show me."

"I've been going over the ship's circuits. It's the only logical place, just like Ahmer said."

Sands nodded Ahmer over, and they watched as Oleg pointed out what he had found.

"Very similar circuitry as the Vestibule. Common electrical here, but this—" he pointed out a tight pattern of cable "—more suitable for data, for computers."

"Could be for medical devices," Ahmer observed. "They basically are computers."

"Yes, but look at this." Oleg pointed to another area. "Servers, maybe?"

"Or massively parallel processors."

"That's what I think." Oleg looked at Sands. "With that kind of computing power, you could run ten ships like *Inferno*, easy. What's it for?"

It was a good question, but Sands felt like he was getting into some high computer geek weeds.

"Sands!" It was Victoria. "Look!"

The overhead screens had lit up with the latest video feed. Sands hadn't heard it, because there was no sound, just images that jumped and pixilated, as if there were some massive atmospheric interference. In fiery block letters was the caption, "WORLD IN CHAOS." It looked like a news report. No news personality was visible, but a subheading, in jarringly jaunty script, read, "Brought to you by Tastes Like Mom's!"

In other circumstances, Sands might have expected Victoria to make some crack about the insipid commercialization of tragedy, but she was silent, her hand to her mouth, her eyes wide with shock.

On screen were images of nuclear destruction, the smoldering rubble of cities under towering mushroom clouds. The first three were Seoul, Pyongyang, and Bashkiristan, the destruction so complete that none were recognizable but for the identifying captions at the bottom of the screen. The fourth city shown was Washington, D.C. The image held for a moment, then swept around, the camera jolting violently before it cut. Sands caught a glimpse through the smoke of white monuments. He hoped that meant the devastation was not complete. Another image was shown, of wreckage in the Sea of Japan, and the loop repeated.

"Is it only those four cities?" Victoria asked.

"We can only pray," Rashid replied.

Victoria looked at Sands. "Did you see at the end...?"

"It looked like the Washington Monument. Maybe the White House. Still standing."

They watched as the loop repeated. The static image of Washington depicted terrible devastation, but it appeared to be a limited area. Sands noticed what looked like an arc of concrete in the foreground.

"That's the Key Bridge," he said. "Georgetown."

"Where's Carrie?" Victoria asked.

"Arlington."

She nodded. Across the Potomac. If the nuclear device wasn't too big, she might have been out of the blast radius.

Catfish put a hand on Sands' shoulder.

"You okay, Bro?"

Sands didn't answer. He glanced around at the monitors, with their rotating video feeds from cameras all over the ship. He turned back to Oleg, gestured at the screens on his console.

"The Psycho Ward. Have we got eyes in there?"

Oleg deferred to Ahmer.

"It's the only place on the ship we don't have the eyes."

***

"Oh, but I have eyes on you."

The one the inmates called Einstein smiled at Sands' perplexed face on one screen among the bank of monitors that ringed his lab on Deck Seven. Dressed in a blood-mottled smock, he worked over a stainless steel table, similar to an autopsy table, but with higher sides, almost like a shallow bathtub. He hummed tunelessly as he picked up a bone saw and worked it with slow, methodical strokes.

A moist black nose edged up to the table and sniffed. Einstein spanked at it playfully with the broad side of his saw.

"Now Cerberus, you know I never give you raw food. You'll get your doggie treat in a minute."

With a final effort, the saw cut through. He set the saw aside, lifted up his specimen, and placed it in a large basin.

What was left on the table was little more than a mass of blood, bone, and gristle. A split ribcage yawned over exposed vertebrae, the cavity emptied of every organ.

Einstein pushed a plunger at the head of the table, and with a whoosh the bottom dropped at an angle, exposing a gaping chute at the foot. The whole mess was washed away with a swirl of water like waste down a toilet. Einstein stripped off his latex surgical gloves and sent them down with the rest.

Humming again, he scrubbed his hands and forearms, all the way up to the elbow.

The animal whined again.

"I haven't forgotten you. Why can't you be as patient as your brothers?" He retrieved three slabs of Process from a container and tossed them one at a time to waiting mouths. "One for you, and one for you, and one for you. No fighting now, plenty for everybody."

The artificial food was slurped down with much snapping and snarling. Einstein hefted the basin in both hands and regarded his latest specimen. It was a human head, severed at the Adam's apple, mouth and eyes frozen in gaping surprise. Einstein smiled, pleased with his handiwork. With mock sympathy, he looked into the dead eyes.

"Alas, poor Fergus."

***

President Stockdale's face glowed an apoplectic red beneath the white frost of his hair. He was huddled in the executive bunker, many fathoms below the White House, with Brzinski, Secretary of State Lum, Secretary of Defense Mallory, and others of his staff. He stood behind his desk, his staff lined up before him like the condemned waiting for the firing squad. Spear and his team looked on from a respectful—and safe—distance.

"You assured me—you *assured* me—Kim's nuclear arsenal would be taken out."

"And it has been, Mr. President." As usual, the others left it to Brzinski to take the lead in these situations. "There was always the contingency that one or two might slip through."

"Well, one did slip through, didn't it? It landed smack dab on Seoul. We haven't heard a word from Park all morning. The very ally we were supposedly protecting!" He turned to Mallory. "And who told you to take out Pyongyang?"

"With all due respect, sir, we couldn't let a strike against Seoul go without a response in kind."

"Well, now we got five mushroom clouds, maybe more to come." He shoved a finger toward the bank of monitors, each showing the same video feed being beamed to *Inferno* and around the world. "That bastard Karga even dropped a bomb on Georgetown!"

Lum spoke up. "Actually, sir, we believe that one was a suitcase bomb."

"I don't care if he smuggled it here in his penny loafers, it's a mother-lovin' mushroom cloud!"

He pointed at another video feed, this one showing the burning wreckage in the Sea of Japan.

"And that ain't no fishin' boat, Mr. Vice President. There were forty thousand men and women on that prison ship."

"Criminals and terrorists," Brzinski icily observed.

"Not to mention we took out two Justice International boats," Mallory added brightly. "We ought to get points for that."

Others laughed, but Stockdale whirled on Mallory with fury. "You think this is a *joke*?"

Mallory had never seen the President in this state. None of them had.

"No, sir."

The President glared at Mallory, the line of the part in his hair as red as a fresh wound. His jaw worked against his clenched teeth, but if he had more to say, he didn't get it out. He plopped into his chair, his rage spent.

When he said no more, Brzinski stepped forward. "Mr. President, if I may. The immediate crisis is over. There will be no more nuclear strikes, because there are no more madmen to launch them."

Stockdale looked his vice president dead in the eye. "I suppose you mean Kim and Karga?"

"Who else?"

"I wonder."

If Brzinski recognized the gibe, he ignored it. "At this moment, Mr. President, the world is holding its breath. Waiting for leadership. *Your* leadership."

Stockdale sighed. "Leadership. How'm I gonna lead from this hole in the ground?"

Stockdale chewed his thumb. His face had gone from red to ashen, his eyes full of doubt. He looked like a man in over his head. Judging from the arch glances exchanged in the room, everyone saw it.

Lum, who had a background in counseling from his pre-political days, dared to put a comforting hand on the old man's shoulder. "You're safe here, sir."

The President harrumphed. With his elbows on his desk, he chafed one fist in the other, his face turned aside. Lum backed away.

Brzinski's eyes weighed Stockdale in the balance. Decisiveness, he firmly believed, was the primary asset of any leader. Quick and confident action. He knew well who among them in the room had it, and who hadn't. He put on his best breezy smile and nodded at the gun and Bible on Stockdale's desk. Picking up on Lum's assurance, his voice took on a hearty tone.

"The President's always safe when he has his trusty forty-four at his side."

A round of chuckles infused the room with good cheer.

"You got that right," Stockdale said with vigor. But there was no cheer in his eyes as he fixed his gaze on Brzinski. "And right now I'm in the mood for some varmint-shootin'."

Brzinski laughed lightly. He looked with admiration on the President's pistol, traced the length of the barrel with his finger. "It is a fine piece. May I?"

Stockdale sat back in his chair and regarded Brzinski like a boss granting an inferior a last wish before giving him the ax. "Go ahead."

Brzinski picked up the gun, turned it over in his hands. "Yes, a fine piece. Do you really keep it loaded?"

Stockdale leaned forward on one elbow, squinted an eye, and affected a John Wayne drawl. "Well, Pilgrim, a gun that's *unloaded* ain't good for nothin'!"

The room filled with sycophantic laughter. Brzinski cut it short by thrusting the gun forward and shooting the President square in the temple.

The shock of the gun blast in the confined space jolted everyone like a slap across the face. Even Brzinski was surprised by its force. The President slumped forward, his head striking the desktop with a liquid thud. No one else moved, not even Spear.

Brzinski eyed the President's lifeless body, the desktop covered with a spray of blood and gore, with something like wonder.

"Well, what do you know," he said. "Old shit-for-brains had brains for brains."

"What have you done," Mallory demanded, his voice a feeble croak.

"Eliminated a problem."

Lum gaped at the bloody spectacle like a nun who had walked in on a priest buggering an altar boy. "But—how will we explain this?"

Brzinski made a quick appraisal. "Lum, you're Korean, aren't you?"

Lum didn't understand the relevance of the question, but after a lifetime of enduring impertinent queries about his heritage, his answer was automatic. "My parents immigrated from Korea, yes."

Brzinski nodded at Spear. Producing a Mac-11 like a rabbit from a hat, Spear cut Lum in two with a burst of fire.

If any of the other civilians in the room had any doubt what the score was, the stances of Spear and his team, weapons in hand, set them straight. They were backing Brzinski.

The former professor scanned his colleagues as he would students at the end of a lecture.

"Any other questions?"

-14-

Damaged people are dangerous. They know they can survive.

—Josephine Hart

Sands marched across the open deck, a duffel of food and water slung over his shoulder, a rifle and ammo under his arm. Victoria came running after him, ahead of the others, who had piled out of the Vestibule to see what was happening.

"Sands! Sands, where are you going?"

"Off this ship."

He came to a lifeboat—a big, enclosed, yellow capsule mounted on a chute that hung over the side. He opened the hatch and tossed his duffle inside.

"There's sixty thousand people on this ship, Sands. What about them?"

"They can fight it out with you over the other twenty-nine lifeboats. Or you can come with me. Your choice."

"Sands, listen to me. Why do you think I was sent here? My father—"

"I don't want to hear your daddy issues."

Victoria's eyes blazed. Sands softened his tone.

"Look, I've got a wife and kid back home. They need me."

"You're kidding yourself, Sands. You lost them a long time ago."

Sands had no answer for that. He picked up the box of ammo from the deck and set it inside the hatch.

"Anybody else coming?"

Catfish, Wolf, and Angel stepped forward.

Angel thumped his chest. "We're with you, hermano."

Sands looked at Ahmer. "How about you, Ahmer?"

Ahmer had taken a step forward, but abruptly stopped. The other Drones, who were inclined to follow him, stopped too. Ahmer scanned their faces, but they gave him no sign, one way or another. He looked back at Sands, but there was no help there, either. Victoria stood firm, her feet spread wide, her arms crossed. Sands noticed that Lani mimicked her stance in female solidarity.

Sands had the sense that Ahmer would follow him, if he made an issue of it, and Lani would follow Ahmer, and pretty soon Victoria would be on the deck alone. All he had to do was say the word, but he told himself he didn't care enough to bother. Anyway, Ahmer needed to decide things for himself.

"Just keep sitting on that pot, Ahmer." To his friends, he said. "Let's go."

Sands turned and put a foot on the rim of the open hatch. A burst of what sounded like gunfire exploded around the lifeboat, and everyone hit the deck. With a creak and a moan of metal grating against metal, the lifeboat separated from its moorings and slid into the sea.

More explosions, from all around the deck, but it wasn't gunfire. It was the exploding bolts that released the couplings holding each lifeboat in place. *Inferno* shed its thirty lifeboats into the sea like a dog shedding fleas. They were soon left behind, a string of yellow bobbers fading into the ship's great wake.

Victoria was the first back on her feet. She met Sands' eyes with a cool smirk. "Looks like I'm not the only one who wants to keep you on this ship."

She turned and sauntered back to the Vestibule. One by one, Ahmer and the other Drones followed.

Catfish clapped Sands on the back. "Tough luck, Bro. For all of us."

Wolf shrugged. "Back to plan B."

Angel added, "I never trusted those little boats anyway."

They went back to join the others, leaving Sands standing there in impotent rage. He gripped his bullpup in his hands, scanning the deck for something to lash out at.

From his lab, Einstein watched in amusement as Sands looked him in the eye and blasted a surveillance camera into oblivion.

***

That night, Sands sat brooding on deck. No one had spoken to him since that afternoon, and that was the way he wanted it. But he wasn't surprised when Ahmer showed up with a plate of noodles he had stirred up in the snack bar.

"I'm not hungry," he said.

"You should eat anyway," Ahmer said, setting the plate down beside him. "The more real food and water you eat the faster the Process will flush out of your system."

Sands grunted, but he left the plate where it lay. Ahmer sat down, and Sands grunted again.

"You have family on the outside." Again, Ahmer had a way of asking a question so that it sounded like a statement.

"Doesn't everybody?"

"I have a mother and two sisters. My father was killed by terrorists."

"So that makes you the man of the family, I guess," Sands said. "Must be nice not to have any competition."

Ahmer frowned at the cruel remark. He sensed there was some deeper significance to it, but he couldn't fathom what it was.

"My mother would sing to us every morning. She would come each to our beds and sing us awake. Very much I would like to hear her voice again."

Sands sighed. "My mom got knocked up behind a club in SoHo by some French guy. Or 'Gee,' I guess you'd say. Shacked up for a while. Thought she was in love. French guy splits. She's so broken up, when I'm born she names me 'Sans.' As in 'without.' Sans Guy Simon, that was the idea. But I guess whoever filled out the birth certificate didn't know French." He shook his head. "She was just a kid. A stupid, selfish kid."

Ahmer considered the story, his expression dour.

"You're not laughing, Ahmer. That's the funniest story I know."

"You think you are a bad man," Ahmer said. "But I do not think you are a bad man."

He got up and walked back to the Vestibule.

"That kid's determined to find your creamy marshmallow center."

Sands craned his neck to find Victoria emerging from the shadows behind him. He stood to meet her, and before Victoria could make another crack, he grabbed her by the wrist.

"I want to talk to you."

He pulled her to a blind spot he had picked out where no surveillance cameras could see. He turned her wrist up to expose the birthmark-like smudge that adorned it.

"We can start with this."

Before she could answer, Sands heard a familiar whistle. It was Catfish, signaling him over to the Vestibule. Sands released his grip on her arm.

"What is it, Cat?"

Victoria followed after Sands, rubbing her wrist, a cryptic glint in her eye.

"We might have a line on that self-destruct device."

Sands entered the Vestibule to find everyone crowded around Bao's console.

"I think we've found the bomb," he said.

On his view screen were two pallets stacked chest high with what looked like brown, paper-wrapped bricks. Rigged between the two pallets was an electronic device with a digital readout.

Wolf said, "If that's C-4, we've got a problem."

There were markings on the packages, but Sands couldn't make them out. "Can you zoom in?"

Bao tapped some keys, and the image grew larger and grainier. But the black lettering was clear enough: C-4.

"Can you get a bead on that readout?"

Bao nudged the camera until the red digital readout was center screen. The device looked something like an old digital clock, its red, squared-off numerals reading 04:06:23 and counting down.

Sands looked at Wolf. Wolf shook his head.

"Where is this, Bao?"

"The Engine room."

"Below decks."

"That's right. Lowest level of the ship."

"You can disarm it, right?" Oleg asked, his eyes shifting from Sands to Wolf and back. "That's part of your training? Disarming bombs?"

"Yeah, two problems with that" Sands replied. "First, we've got to go through nine circles of hell just to get to it, and whoever is pulling the strings isn't about to make that easy on us."

"How do you know?" Desmond asked. "Maybe he doesn't want to be blown to bits either."

Lani nodded her agreement. "Maybe he doesn't even know about the bomb."

"Maybe. Or maybe he knows, and doesn't care. He's got us trapped on board without those lifeboats. Or maybe he's got other arrangements."

Victoria broke in on the speculation. "What's the other problem?"

Wolf nodded at the screen. "That ain't no pipe bomb. We get to it, we probably can't disarm it."

Angel pointed at a fuzzy area of the timing mechanism. "That looks like a radio receiver right there."

Sands looked close. "Yeah. Maybe a fail-safe? To Oleg, he said, "What have you got on the Psych Ward?"

"The only surveillance on Deck Seven covers the outer ring of cells, where you were this morning." Oleg pulled up a schematic on one of the screens. "The Psych Ward itself makes up the center of the deck, and it's a totally dark area. There's the Arena, too, but the lights and cameras are always dark except when a Battle is scheduled. We can't access them from here."

"So what's the theory? Who's in charge?"

The Drones did their routine of exchanging silent looks again, but this time Sands knew what they were thinking.

"Einstein."

Victoria asked, "Einstein?"

"That's what the Dregs call him." Sands turned to the Drones. "You guys must know his real name."

Shrugs and shaking heads.

"So who is he?"

Bao went to his console, tapping keys. "He's not crew and he's not inmate. We can't find him anywhere in the manifest. The only time we ever see him is during Battle. He watches the fights from an observation deck over the Arena. They say he runs the Psycho Ward."

Bao pulled up an image that looked like it might have been captured from a video feed. "Everybody calls him Einstein, even the crew."

Seeing the image, Victoria gasped.

"You know. Because of the hair."

Sands looked at Victoria. The expression on her face had nothing to do with Einstein's hair. "What is it?"

"I know him."

Everyone looked at her.

"One of my father's old partners. A friend of the family. His name's Buddy Henderson."

"Buddy Henderson?" Sands turned the name over in his mind. "Why do I know that name?"

Lani said, "Isn't that the Tastes Like Mom's guy?"

"Holy shit! He used to do those commercials with his mother." Bao laughed. "They were funny."

Sands nodded, the scattered pieces of memory fitting back together. "The inventor of Process."

-15-

Governments exist to protect the rights of minorities. The loved and the rich need no protection—they have many friends and few enemies.

—Wendell Phillips

Sands grabbed Victoria again by the wrist and dragged her out of the Vestibule, away from electronic eyes. Once they were out of sight she snatched her arm away.

"I'm not used to being manhandled."

"So start talking."

"Don't do it again. You might not like what happens next."

Tough talk for a former student government nerd, Sands thought, but he could see she was serious. "Fair enough."

If she wanted an apology, she didn't get one. This wasn't the Sands she used to know, the one she could embarrass with a flirty look back at Stanford.

"I don't know where to begin…"

"Start with Einstein."

She smiled thinly. "Uncle Buddy. That's what we used to call him, even my father. Whenever he visited the house he'd bring Todd and me some crazy treat he'd cooked up in his laboratory—licorice flavored spaghetti, bananas that tasted like ice cream."

"So the Doctor was interested in that kind of stuff?"

"Not really. Not at first, anyway. But Uncle Buddy had a way of taking the most outlandish ideas and making them real. Like, you might think an exploding walnut is a stupid idea, but they make perfect little grenades. Imagine a terrorist carrying a bagful of them through airport security right onto a plane."

"I'd rather imagine how you're telling me stuff I need to know."

"The point is, Father saw how useful Uncle Buddy could be. He loved to feed him ideas, just to see what he would do with them. But Father could never control him. The trick was always to let him do his work without risking him going freelance."

"So Dr. Brzinski locks him away here, but gives him free reign over his own Frankenstein's laboratory."

"My father's insane. You saw what he tried to do to me."

"Come on, what could daddy's little girl possibly do to get him to turn on you like that?"

"Please. My father suffered me for two reasons only. He respected my intelligence and he thought he could use me to lure you into the fold." Victoria's face reddened. "I only played along because..." She looked away.

Sands had never seen Victoria vulnerable before—at least not when she had full possession of her faculties. She had always been so calculated in her emotional displays, he wondered if he could trust it.

"Why? Why did your father want me?"

"Because you're everything Todd is not. Everything my Father is not, for that matter. My father worships strength. He wanted Thor for a son, but what he got was Loki. When you betrayed him—"

"I never did."

"In his eyes, you did. Anyway, I'd say you broke his heart, if I thought he had a heart."

"So what did you do? To break his heart?"

"There was a plot against his life."

"You knew about it? And you didn't tell him?"

"I was part of it."

Sands chewed on that. He wondered what could make a child turn against her own father. To want him dead. Even a father like Henry Brzinski.

"You were supposed to be sent to the Psych Ward, weren't you? Ahmer picked up on that. But somebody interfered."

"We have friends on the inside."

Sands took her wrist—gently this time, and turned it up. "Is that what this is? The guy we raided in Bashkiristan—he had one too."

Victoria shook her head. She took out a pen-size UV light and clicked it. The smudge came to life, projecting the complex, three-dimensional geometric figure that Ahmer had shown him in the cell.

"The 600 Cell. You might remember my father had a mock-up of one on his desk."

"I do remember. I noticed it the first time he asked me into his study. I saw it in Bashkiristan, too, but it didn't mean anything to me."

"And on the ship."

"Yeah, now that you mention it."

"It's the emblem of a secret organization that's infiltrated the world's major powers, a global shadow government."

"And your father—he pulls the strings?"

Victoria snapped off the pen light. The sparkling emblem vanished.

"Not alone, not yet, but he's been positioning himself for years for a complete takeover. Karga was the bank."

"But Karga started to get ideas."

"Father loves ideas—except when other people have them. The 600 Cell was never designed to be ruled by one individual, but with the U.S. government under Father's control, nobody will be able to stand against him. The New Freedom Party was an important step. Instead of ruling behind the scenes, he wants his hands on the controls."

"And Force—is that part of it? Me, Catfish, G.K., the whole thing?"

Victoria put a hand on his arm. "Don't take it too hard. Half the people working for The 600 are just patriotic grunts doing their duty."

Sands knew she didn't mean to be unkind, but the words stung nevertheless.

"Back to Uncle Buddy. What does all this have to do with *Inferno*?"

Victoria chewed her lip as she mulled over the ill-fitting pieces of the puzzle. "I think maybe Process is the key."

"Process? You're kidding. It's just another way to make money by getting people to eat crap."

"Sure, but think about it. On one level, Process is just what they say it is—a way to recycle organic waste into cheap, high-protein food. But it's chemicals. They can manipulate them any way they want."

Sands wasn't getting it.

"Look, the real breakthrough with Process is that it doesn't contain any flavoring. It bypasses the flavor receptors to work directly on the brain. It's a drug."

"So we're guinea pigs. A controlled experiment."

"That's part of what the different decks are about, I think. Each level gets a different chemical configuration."

"But why? What's the 600 Cell care about getting people to buy more junk food?"

"Think about it, Sands. The 600 Cell wants world domination. And if they can control people's minds through the food they eat, you can bet they're not going to settle for making people think sawdust tastes like meatloaf."

***

The blind spot Sands had found for his private talk with Victoria wasn't as private as he thought. Einstein was able to watch them from a camera on the other side of the deck, although it was too far away to hear what was being said. He tried zooming in close enough to lip read—one of the many odd skills he had picked up over the years—but it was too far away for that, too. No matter—he felt confident that anything they cooked up he would be able to handle.

It did irk him, though, to see them so blatantly plotting against him, so sure of themselves that he couldn't overhear. He watched as the one called Sands strode back to the Vestibule to retrieve one of the Drones. Which one? He checked his roster—the one called Ahmer. The names of his subjects were of no real consequence, but Einstein was obsessive about details, and he always liked to know the names of his adversaries. Enemies without names were so much less satisfying to kill.

After an animated discussion that ended with emphatic nodding from the Drone, the three of them marched back to the Vestibule. Einstein had dozens of eyes there, and he waited with much interest to see what they would do.

Once in the Vestibule, though, it was all whisper and mime, passing whatever plan they had devised rom Drone to Drone. After a moment, the Drones were all rummaging through tool boxes and supply cabinets. What was it they were gathering? Tape. Electrical tape, masking tape, duct tape. Einstein couldn't imagine what they were going to do with it, but once everyone in the Vestibule had a roll, they all set about their work.

Einstein quickly realized they were covering up the cameras and yanking out the microphone jacks, rendering him blind and deaf. One by one he watched each camera go dark. He wouldn't have believed they could get them all, but the Drones were clever little techies, and somehow they managed to ferret out every one. Every mic went dead, too, and he watched glumly as the Drone called Ahmer approached the final camera, duct tape in hand, as if he meant to slap it right across Einstein's face. All was black.

Cerberus gave out a belligerent bark, sensing his master's mood. Einstein reached down to find an ear and scratched it, contemplating his next move.

***

"Okay," Sands began, once everyone had gathered around. "Now that we've got some privacy, we can talk."

Sands repeated what he and Victoria had discussed, emphasizing that their top priority was to disarm the bomb. "But frankly, I don't think there's any way Einstein, or whoever is pulling the strings from the Psycho Ward, is going to let us get near that device. We'll have to take him out first."

Catfish nodded his agreement. "If he lets all the Psychs loose, though, we're going to need more weapons."

"And explosives," Wolf added. "If Einstein hunkers down in some hidey-hole, they might come in handy."

Sands smiled wide. "Boys, we got all the bang-bang your little hearts could ever desire."

"What I'm still not getting," Angel said, "is why they wanna blow up the ship. What's that get them?"

"That might be the good news," Sands replied. "It shows The 600 aren't confident they can pull this off—not if they're exposed."

Seeing the doubtful looks, Victoria elaborated. "There are seven black rafts—six, now that the one in the Sea of Japan has been taken out. Until now, they've just been a Justice International conspiracy theory. But it's not easy to keep that kind of thing covered up, and this nuclear outbreak has shaken The 600's grip. The people may have been all for the prison ships when it came to actual criminals and terrorists, but the black rafts are run for profit. Supply and demand. They need bodies to fill those cells, but if you scoop up too many innocent neighbors and family members, people start to notice."

"So what?" Oleg said. "If The 600 are so powerful, what do they care what people think?"

Sands and Victoria had the same thought, both recalling lessons from Dr. Brzinski. Sands gave it voice.

"'There is no despot so powerful that he does not govern by the consent of his people.'"

"What's that," Angel asked. "Philosophy?"

"'No. Observable fact.'" Victoria smiled wryly. "We're quoting my father. Just like old school days, huh, Sands?"

Oleg wasn't having it. "Bullshit, people agree to dictators. I lived under a dictator. You think I wanted to?"

"North Korea is the most militarized nation in modern history," Sands answered, citing one of the Doctor's favorite examples. "But its military only makes up one-twentieth of the total population. Even if you count everyone in the reserves, the police, and the secret police, civilians outnumber government forces four, maybe five to one. You think they couldn't toss Kim out on his ear if they really wanted to?"

Oleg thought about it. "I still say bullshit."

"Okay," Catfish put in. "So the ships are a political embarrassment. But they're worth billions. You tellin' me they're just gonna flush all that money down the toilet?"

Victoria shrugged. "These are privately owned ships, financed and insured by government debt. If we happen to hit an iceberg, so what? Everybody gets paid."

"And the taxpayer foots the bill," Catfish concluded.

Angel spread his hands. "Sounds like the American way to me."

"Is class over now?" Wolf asked. "It ain't politics that's gonna blow up the ship. It's the bomb. And the clock's ticking."

-16-

God how the dead men
Grin by the wall,
Watching the fun of the Victory Ball.

—Alfred Noyes

After a quick trip back to the magazine for more armaments, Sands and his three Force compadres returned to find that the Drones had worked out a plan. They had hung sheets off the cots from the ceiling, closing off one end of the Vestibule, and projected the schematics for *Inferno* on a blank wall. Everyone crammed into the little area, finding seats on scavenged chairs, boxes, or whatever space they could find on the floor. Ahmer stood beside the impromptu projection screen, a self-conscious presenter holding forth with a shaky laser pointer.

"The problem we have is, even if we can make our plans secret from Einstein, when we step outside the Vestibule he can see every move we make."

He pointed out the elevator shaft. "The elevators are under surveillance. Cameras inside, cameras outside the doors on every deck."

"So we knock out the cameras," Angel suggested.

"There are too many. Even here in the Vestibule we cannot be sure we have blocked every camera."

"That's why we're under cover," Bao explained. "We'd need a week to scan the whole Vestibule for eyes and ears, but this storage area should be secure."

"Even if we knock out the cameras in the elevators," Ahmer continued, "Einstein still can track their operation. He knows when we use them, or what deck we go to. But if we don't use the elevators—if we use the shafts—he can't track us so easy."

"Shafts?" Victoria asked. "You mean the elevator shafts?"

"Yes."

Sands nodded appreciatively. "Not bad, kid."

"Wait," Bao said. "There's more."

Ahmer held up a key. "This key overrides the elevators' automatic controls. The only way Einstein can stop us to use it is to shut off the power. If he does that, the elevators return to maintenance positions, below decks."

Catfish raised his hand as he would at a formal briefing. Ahmer was surprised by the gesture, but he managed what Sands thought was a very professorial nod.

"That's where we want to go anyway, isn't it? I mean, that's where the bomb is."

"Yes, elevator maintenance is one deck below the engine room. But if Einstein could seal the hatch of the maintenance well, anyone on the elevators would be trapped."

Wolf flipped a packet of C-4 in the air and caught it with a flourish. "So we blow the hatch."

"That would not be advisable in such confined space," Ahmer answered, bringing up an image of the well.

Wolf shrugged. "I'll use thermite, then."

"Yes, but if we trick Einstein into shutting the power, he thinks we are trapped. This gives us an advantage."

***

From his spider's nest on Deck Seven, Einstein watched with keen interest as Sands, Catfish, Angel, and Wolf came bursting out of the Vestibule, bristling with arms and sheathed in body armor. They double-timed it to the elevator, where Sands punched the call button as two others stood guard, guns ready for whatever may come. The fourth man, Einstein was amused to see, took out a can of spray paint scavenged from stores and blotted out the camera.

Blind to their movements for only a second, he picked them up again as they entered the elevator. As the one called Angel shook his can of spray paint, Einstein caught a glimpse of Sands flashing a metal key and inserting it into the control panel. Too slow by an instant, Angel sprayed the camera lens, and the interior image went fuzzy and dark. Einstein smiled and shook his head.

"Sloppy, sloppy."

What he did not see was Wolf popping open the maintenance hatch in the elevator's ceiling. Wolf climbed up and into the shaft, followed by Catfish and Sands. Wolf secured one end of a rope and dropped the other through the hatch, to Angel, who secured it to a harness around his waist. He gave Sands a thumbs up. The others likewise signaled their readiness, and Sands said, "Hit it!"

Angel punched the bottom button, and the elevator started down, dropping away as he was pulled by the rope through the hatch and left dangling in the air. Sands

grabbed the taught rope and swung Angel over to a foot-
hold. Once he was secure, they all watched as the elevator
car sank down into the darkness.

"Let's see if he takes the bait," Sands said.

In his lab, Einstein watched the indicator light on his
master control panel as it tracked the elevator's progress,
blinking Deck Two, Deck Three, Deck Four...

"Where are you going, little men?"

The indicator blinked past Deck Nine.

"Below decks." Quickly, Einstein threw a switch, then
several others in quick succession. "And there you'll stay."

As Sands and his party clung to their handholds, there
was the jolt and whine of turbines powering down, and
the mechanical clatter of all the ship's elevators as they
started downward, carried to the bottoms of their shafts
by their own weight.

Sands spoke into a radio on his shoulder. "Ahmer, you
read me?"

"Ahmer here."

"Einstein bought it." There was a long pause. "Ahmer?"

"Repeat, please?"

Sands rolled his eyes. "That means it worked."

"Oh, that's good."

"Radio silence. We're going down. Out."

The elevator shaft had a single ladder that ran from top
to bottom, bolted to the interior girders. Angel, already
below the others, led the way. Although there was no surveillance within the shaft, its structure was only partially
enclosed, leaving the climbers exposed at times to anyone
who might be looking. The semidarkness that enveloped
the whole ship, darker still in the shaft, worked to their
advantage. It was slow going, but they climbed steadily

down, one after the other, descending past the stenciled legends that marked each deck, all the way to seven.

Reaching their destination, Angel shifted his feet from the ladder to the narrow ledge at deck level, inching out of the way to make room for Sands and the others. Wolf came last, and he regarded the bulkhead legend **7 VIO-LENCE 7** with a mordant smile.

"That's what you call foreshadowing."

Sands thumbed the safety on his weapon and threw the bolt. The others followed suit.

"When we go through those doors we'll be exposed to live surveillance. Let's hope Einstein is taking a coffee break."

He gave the signal. Angel jimmied the doors, and they were in.

***

It wasn't coffee Einstein was having in his quarters adjacent to the Psycho Ward lab, but the Process equivalent of fried chicken. He was packing equipment and personal items into a case, pausing now and again to sample one of the rectangular slabs from a tray on his bed, licking his fingers between each bite and wiping them on his pants.

There was a monitor in his quarters, but he wasn't watching it. The screen simultaneously showed four images that rotated among the many cameras on Violence Deck. Confident he had stymied the Drone insurgency, and preoccupied with preparations for his own escape, he didn't notice the images of four armed men flitting across the screen as they made their way out of the elevator shaft to the Deck Seven mezzanine.

As he thumbed through a folder of notes, a poster over his desk caught his eye. It was an old Tastes Like Mom's ad, depicting a younger and better-groomed Garrick "Buddy" Henderson, bending down to sample a bite proffered by his adorable little mom. Thinking about his mom always brought back happy memories, but he didn't smile wistfully or hold back a tear or even particularly notice her. He gazed instead at the younger version of himself, mentally comparing the image to the man he was now. It wasn't just that he was older, or that his milky complexion had turned sallow and pockmarked. The young Buddy Henderson was tall and gangly, his shoulders narrow, his muscles underdeveloped. With his frizz of black hair, thin face, and prominent nose, he looked like some sort of strange, featherless bird. His hair was graying now, and although he no longer consciously cultivated his commercial "brand" of the quirky, bow-tied scientist, it was just as wild. His face had become broader, as had his shoulders, but he wasn't fat. His arms and legs had become thick with muscle and sinew. He looked at his hands. They had once been the delicate appendages of a sequestered academic, but they were thick and rough now. He picked up a metal drinking cup, the kind that—because of its potential as an improvised weapon—was strictly forbidden among the inmates. It was surprising, even to him, how easily he could crush it.

As he contemplated the collapsed aluminum cylinder in his hand, an image on the monitor behind him went bright white with the flare of a thermite charge. Cerberus, who had been dozing in a corner, perked up, its eyes watching the flare go dim. Four dark figures appeared in the waning glow, threw back the blown hatch, and scrambled through before the image cycled to another view of the deck.

Cerberus whined and barked, but by the time Einstein turned to look, he saw nothing on the monitor but four images of stillness, cycling through their regular rotation.

"Now, now," he said, tossing slabs of artificial chicken across the room to three eager mouths. "Hasn't Daddy taught you not to beg?"

***

The flare from the thermite charge Wolf used to breach the entrance to the Psycho Ward was so bright it dazzled them even with shielded eyes. The open hatch gaped like the black mouth of a bottomless pit, but they couldn't stand in the open waiting for their eyes to adjust, and they didn't want to risk drawing attention to themselves by using their torches. Sands forged ahead.

Once they were in, it only took a moment before their eyes recovered and details of the chamber began to emerge. The overhead lights were off, but running lights along the floor glowed dimly, showing the way between two long rows of cages. The only other light came from the series of green LEDs that indicated each cage was secure.

Most of the cages were small ones in stacks, populated with rats and monkeys, but there were larger cages as well, with chimpanzees and even pigs. Except for the rustle of movement and a wheezing pant somewhere down the line, the chamber was completely quiet. Sands wondered if most of the animals weren't dead.

"Cristo!" Angel crossed himself and kissed the gold crucifix that hung from his neck. "I thought this kind of animal experiment shit was against the law."

The others gave Angel a look that made him wish he had kept quiet. Sands signaled them forward.

As they progressed down the line it became apparent these were no ordinary animals and they had been subjected to no ordinary experiments. In the shadows the men could make out misshapen creatures, some with too many legs, some with too few, some with strange growths and artificial appendages. They averted their eyes, focusing on the twin lines of running lights that would lead them out.

Someone said, "We're gonna burn this motherfucker to the ground when we get through."

The next hatch they came to was shut but unsecured. A quick scan showed no alarms, and Sands clicked the latch and eased it open. All clear. They couldn't get through fast enough.

The second chamber was much like the first, but the cages were larger and they were all filled with men.

"Guinea pigs," Sands breathed.

"You say something?"

Sands answered Catfish with a gesture forward.

Like the men in the cages they had encountered on their way to rescue Wolf, these men were no ordinary prisoners; they were experimental subjects. But whatever experiments they were undergoing, these men must have been further along in the process. Their shapes and faces were outsized and distorted, afflicted with some form of gigantism. Most looked human enough, but Sands caught glimpses of some grotesques that would have put Bloody-face to shame. They muttered, they keened, they screamed. But no one talked. Not words.

Sands, Catfish, and Angel tried not to make eye contact, tried not to even look. But Wolf would not turn away. This could have been his future.

"We open these cages," Sands said, "something tells me we won't be greeted as liberators."

Wolf's eyes showed his agreement.

The keening and wailing from the Psychs grew louder, the presence of outsiders stirring them up. Sands double-timed it, but this only agitated them more. They came to the next hatch, also latched but unsealed, and wasted no time in getting through and closing it behind them.

They were in the lab now. The overhead lights, on re-serve power, were dimmed, and the place glowed in a twi-light of video monitors, electronic displays, and LEDs. The first thing Sands noticed were the three autopsy ta-bles. Fortunately, each of them was unoccupied, the stain-less steel clean and gleaming.

Catfish pointed to an area on the right. "Look there. Looks like his command center."

They moved in for a closer look. They saw the bank of video monitors, the big captain's chair that swiveled amongst an array of controls.

"This is it, all right," Wolf said. "Looks like he's got con-trol of the whole ship, right here at his fingertips."

He punched a button. "Deck Nine." The monitors de-picted a multitude of views of Treachery Deck. He punched another, with the same result. "Deck Eight." The images were all quiet, everyone in their cells. "Let's see how the Vestibule looks." He punched another button, but this time all the screens came up blank, except two. One was of the exterior of the Vestibule, which the Drones had not blacked out, since it was their eyes on their own immediate vicinity.

"Not bad," Catfish observed. "Looks like we just about got them all. But what's that one there?"

The image was of Hari, staring intently into the camera, his face bathed in a warm glow. The glow subsided, and he pulled back a door, reached in, and came back with a bowl of noodles.

"Microwave," Wolf said. "Sneaky bastards put a camera in the microwave."

Angel caught Sands staring into space.

"What is it, Sands?"

Sands was looking past the bank of monitors to the balcony from which Einstein would observe the battles in the Arena. He had always taken a special interest in Sands' battles. How many times had Sands looked up from the Arena floor to see Einstein staring down on him? He tried to remember the number of kills the emcee had credited him for. He didn't like to keep track himself.

"Sands?"

"Mm?" Sands snapped out of his reverie. "Nothing. Let's move on."

Wolf caught Sands by the sleeve. "Sands, we've got what we need right here. If we keep Einstein out, he can't do shit. Two men oughta be able to hold him off. The other two can go disarm the bomb."

Sands thought about it, but it was no go. "First of all, we don't know what Einstein can do. Second, we're not splitting up until we find him."

Wolf checked his watch. Or Desmond's watch, since that's who he had taken it from. "We're cutting it close, Cap."

"We'd better move then."

They made their way back past the autopsy tables, coming to a series of what looked like incubators, each containing a different human organ, some floating in amber-colored baths, others suspended among a tangle of tubes that appeared to be filled with blood and other organic liquids.

Sands stopped cold before an incubator that contained a suspended human head. It stood mounted on a stainless steel rod that must have been fixed to the spine, the cranium held upright by a crown of smaller rods bolted to the forehead and back. A webwork of tubes large and small fed into the neck, cycling blood and lymph in a pulsing flow like a slow heartbeat. The eyes were closed, the flesh as ruddy as if alive.

"Fergus."

Angel crossed himself again.

"You know him, Sands?"

"Yeah. Lucky bastard got paroled to Limbo Deck."

"Guess he didn't make it."

Sands was a praying man, of sorts, but he wasn't the type to offer up pleas for the souls of the departed. He stared at Fergus' dead face with little feeling but queasiness.

But then Fergus stared back. His eyes snapped open and fixed on Sands like a man startled out of sleep. His mouth worked in silent speech.

Everyone—that is, everyone but Wolf—jumped back in startled fright. Sands jumped back so suddenly he knocked over a standing rack of biometric monitors. It hit the floor with a crash.

In Einstein's quarters, the head of a Chihuahua perked up at the sound, muffled by bulkheads but still distinct. Two giant mastiffs followed. The Chihuahua growled.

"What is it, Cerberus?" Einstein thought he had heard something too. He put aside his packing and turned his attention to the surveillance monitor.

In the lab, Sands and his crew had come to the hatch that led to Einstein's living quarters. It was a large, metal door—large enough for a seven-foot-tall man to step through without stooping—with a single lever to open it.

Wolf tried the latch. "This one's sealed."

On the door frame next to the lever was a red button, under which was the single word "OPEN."

"Should we try the button?" Angel asked.

Catfish replied, "So Einstein can buzz us in?"

"Better blow it," Sands said.

Wolf nodded his assent and applied thermite to the latch and hinges. "Fire in the hole," he announced as everyone took cover. "Five, four, three, two..."

The images on Einstein's monitor cycled through to the lab just in time to catch the thermite charge. As the men on the monitor converged on the compromised hatch, Cerberus leapt to its four feet, its massive chest contracting in sharp spasms as its three grafted-on heads barked warning.

Einstein pointed in the direction of the lab. "Cerberus, to the lab. Attack!"

The creature galloped away, its slavering mastiff heads emitting low growls, its Chihuahua head yipping madly.

In the lab, the hatch was compromised but still firmly in place. Sands gripped the latch as Angel and Catfish positioned pry-bars on either side.

"On three. One, two—"

The lights went out.

Catfish said, "Uh-oh." With his ear almost to the bulkhead, he thought he heard the sound of something approaching on the other side.

"Pull it," Sands ordered. "Now!"

"Sands, wait—"

The hatch burst open. Cerberus charged through, bowling over the three men at the door. Sands was pinned beneath the heavy slab of metal, pummeled as feet seemed to jump up and down upon it with the intent of pounding him through the deck. He heard the snaps and snarls of a wolf pack. He heard shouts and screams. Something bit him above the ankle with such force he could feel the teeth through his body armor. He struggled free, lashing out at the beast with his knife, but he only struck metal. Someone got off some shots. There was a yelp, and the beast was gone.

"What the holy fuck was that!" Angel was on his hands and knees, panting, a tendril of blood making its way down one arm.

Catfish sat flat on his backside, his smoking bullpup propped in his lap. "I think I hit it. I couldn't hardly see."

Sands struggled to his feet, his one leg throbbing. He turned his torch on it. He could see where the teeth had pierced the armor, but he didn't see any blood. Probably he had a bruise, nothing more.

"Where's Wolf?"

Sands swept the darkness with his flash. A glimpse of red. "Wolf!"

They scrambled over to him. He was on his back, his hands to his neck, thick gouts of blood flowing over his fingers. Catfish snagged a roll of gauze from a cabinet.

Sands took hold of Wolf's wrists and, looking him in the eye, eased his hands away.

"Easy, Bro, easy."

Resisting at first, Wolf let his hands fall away. A long, jagged wound exposed the white of his trachea. His torn jugular pulsed red. Sands took the gauze and tried to stanch the bleeding, packing the wound as fast as he could. Catfish took one of Wolf's hands, Angel the other, as Sands continued to press the wound, but the blood was coming too fast. Wolf looked at each of his three comrades and tried to speak, but only bubbles of blood came to his lips.

"We're here, Bro," Angel told him, chafing his hand. "We're here."

Wolf squeezed once, and his hand went limp.

Catfish passed his hand over Wolf's eyes, pressing the lids closed.

The men bowed their heads in grief, but there was no time to mourn. A thunderous buzzer sounded in staccato bursts. They gaped at each other, knowing it could only mean one thing—the Psycho Ward cells were opening en masse.

"Let's go," Sands said quietly. He and Angel rose and began their retreat, but Catfish lingered. The Psychs were already at the lab entrance. "Catfish! Let's go!"

Catfish laid a hand on Wolf's shoulder. "We'll be back for you, Brother."

-17-

If you're going through hell, keep going.
—Winston Churchill

"Go! Go! Go!"

The Psychs were through the hatch. As Catfish set out at a dead run, Sands pitched a flash-bang over his head, bouncing it into the middle of the pack. It slowed them, but they kept coming. He waited at the hatch into the main quarters for Catfish to get through, and slid two more flash-bangs across the deck into their midst. The Psychs wailed in confusion and anger. Some blindly thrashed about the lab, sending incubators flying. Others were hardly fazed.

Sands signaled Angel and Catfish forward. He pulled the broken hatch back against the portal to slow down the Psychs, but it was wasted effort. Looking back as he ran, he saw that they scarcely missed a step as they tossed it aside. There was a shout from Angel.

"There he goes!"

Up ahead they caught a glimpse of Einstein slipping through another hatch, Cerberus at his heels, its three heads snapping and snarling wildly. Sands and the others charged after him, but Einstein paused to lay down a spray of machine-gun fire that sent them diving for cover.

With no damage done, they sprang back to their feet and picked up the pursuit, zigging and zagging through the maze of passageways. Einstein had the advantage of a head start, but he was slowed by the large case he was carrying. Feeling the pressure, he wildly sprayed fire over his shoulder as he ran. But Sands and his men were in a squeeze, too. With every turn, they gained on Einstein, but the Psychs also gained on them. It wasn't enough for Sands to lay down cover fire—the Psychs didn't respond to threat the way a normal human would. Unless they were hit, they just kept coming.

As Einstein slipped through yet another hatch, not even thirty feet ahead of them, Sands needed back-up. The Psychs were piling through a hatch faster than he could take them out. Angel and Catfish threw down with their own bull-pups, laying down a curtain of fire that even the Psychs could not withstand. From the caterwauling on the other side, Sands knew they hadn't fully retreated, but they would have to shove a lot of bodies out of the way to get back through.

They had lost sight of Einstein, and the next hatch led to an area in near-total darkness. They eased their way through, weapons at the ready. Sands slammed the hatch shut behind them and jimmied it with a pry-bar. In the back of his mind was the half-formed question of why Einstein had not bothered to do the same, why he had not sealed any of the hatches behind him as he ran.

"There, up ahead." Angel pointed out a dim light.

"I see it."

They double-timed it down a long corridor, coming to an open space. The light they had seen from the other end of the corridor came from a single spot that hung from a high ceiling. It created a well of light surrounded by darkness that obscured the boundaries of whatever chamber they were in. There was nothing to indicate a way out. Even the corridor from which they had come was invisible in the gloom.

"Where the hell are we?" Catfish asked.

Recognition dawned on Sands just as dazzling lights came up and the clang of slamming metal gates sounded all around them. They were in the Arena.

The three men instinctively aligned themselves back-to-back-to-back, guns at the ready. On six sides of the octagonal Arena, shouting, gibbering Psychs clamored at the gates, each shoving and tearing at the others, like starving predators eager to get at their prey. Only two or three at a time could squeeze their way up against the narrow openings, but in the chutes behind, Sands could see more pressing their way forward.

Sands cast about for an exit, and at nine o'clock he recognized the "challenger's cage," the very one he had occupied many times. Its chute did not lead back to the Psycho Ward but to the main elevator. It was empty. He pointed.

"There. That's the way out."

They ran up to it, their sudden movement arousing the clamor of the Psychs to an even higher pitch. Sands tested the lock. It was sealed. He looked at the others.

"Please tell me Wolf didn't have all of the thermite."

Catfish said, "All I've got are grenades and flash-bangs."

Angel shrugged. "Me too."

Sands grimaced. "We'll have to blow it with a grenade."

"Are you crazy?" Catfish waved his arm over the empty space that surrounded them. "We've got no cover."

The Psychs tugged and pounded at the gates, trying to tear them out with their bare hands. The whole structure of the Arena was vibrating.

"We can duck back out the way we came," Angel suggested.

"No we can't." Sands nodded at the gate through which they had entered, now sealed and straining against the weight of a half-dozen Psychs.

Starting with a low rumble and rising to a volume that drowned out even the Psychs, a booming voice filled the Arena:

"A-A-R-R-R-E YOU R-R-R-R-R-E-A-D-D-Y-Y FOR B-A-A-A-A-T-T-L-L-L-L-E!"

The recording of the familiar cry of the Arena emcee incited the Psychs to a wild chant of "BAT-TLE! BAT-TLE!" Some managed to sound convincingly human in their enunciation, while others merely screamed or pounded their fists in time. The jumbotron flared to life, ringing the Arena with images of Einstein's leering face.

The same happened in the Vestibule. Victoria, Rashid, and the Drones watched in stunned silence as half the monitors were filled with Einstein's face, half with images of the Psychs and the three men in the Arena. Ahmer was surprised to find Lani gripping his hand.

"That was a very neat trick with the elevator." Einstein's voice rasped through electronic static. "Too bad I didn't have more time to work with you boys..." He cocked his head, and his eyes zeroed in on the two women in the Vestibule with uncanny perception. "And girls. I could have done for you what I've done for the Psychs."

"Back at you—*Ein-stein*." Sands elongated the nickname for maximum aggravation. "I've killed a lot of Psychs. I'll be happy to add you to the list."

The barb hit home. Einstein's sallow face boiled purple with anger. But he managed a hangman's smile. "You're good at one-on-one combat, Sands. Let's see how you do at battle royal."

His image retreated, and the screens were filled with the three slavering heads of Cerberus before all went black.

"What the hell was that?" Victoria exclaimed.

Desmond crossed himself. Rashid clapped his hands together in prayer. The screens came back up, showing every angle in the Arena. The three men—surrounded by dozens of screaming psychopaths—stood in half-crouches, guns poised, their eyes juiced wide by nerves jangling with flight-or-fight impulses. As the staccato burst of the warning buzzer counted down to the release of the Psychs, Rashid spoke his prayer aloud. Ahmer listened, his Arabic too poor to join in, though he seconded the words in his heart: "O Allah, we ask You to restrain them by their necks, and we seek refuge in You from their evil!"

In the Arena, Sands and his men turned their backs to the wall, spreading themselves apart just enough to give each a clear line of fire. The buzzer counted down—six, five, four—and Sands leveled his rifle.

"I don't feature waitin'" he growled—a favorite expression of G.K.'s—and he pounded one of the gates with a burst from his bullpup. Psychs wailed, spun, and fell as bullets ricocheted off the steel mesh and into the chute. Catfish and Angel instantly followed Sands' example, each targeting a separate gate. A dozen Psychs went down, wounded or dead.

If only they had thought of the tactic sooner. The last, long blast of the buzzer sounded and the gates belched out their mindless furies.

The moment of shock felt by Victoria and the Drones at what amounted to the cold-blooded murder of defenseless men in cages was swept away by the horror of the battle that followed. Sands, Catfish, and Angel lay down a withering hail of fire, but the Psychs kept coming—limbs ripped away, torsos riddled, bodies stacking up like a revetment of flesh and bone—nothing stopped them but death.

Magazines emptied, and still they came. The instant it took to drop one mag and jam in another was all it took for several Psychs to close the gap, and the fight was down to pistols and knives.

Catfish managed to get off one last blast from his bullpup, taking the legs out from one charging Psych, but the crazed beast's momentum carried him forward, and he wrapped Catfish up like a linebacker. Catfish struck down with his rifle butt, beating his attacker's brains to jelly before the clawing and biting ceased.

Angel almost got wrapped up by another, but he was able to put a knife in his eye. The Psych collapsed like a puppet with its strings cut. Sands got the same result planting a nine millimeter slug through a Psych's ear. Headshots, they realized, were the most effective. Although the Psych's bodies were able to withstand superhuman levels of abuse, like any mere mortal coils they needed brains to make them go.

Sands heard Angel scream, but a Psych had him from behind, and he was struggling to knife him wherever he could reach. Catfish was down to fists, straddling a kicking, flailing Psych as he pummeled him with everything he had.

Out of the corner of his eye, Sands saw Angel being dragged away by four or five Psychs to the far end of the Arena. Another half dozen joined in, ripping at him with ragged teeth and nails. Catfish broke free from his attacker and charged across the Arena, launching himself at the backs of the Psychs that had Angel on the deck. Sands slashed out with his knife with such force that it cut his own foe's neck clear to the spine. He ran to join the fray, but he feared he was too late.

Catfish had finished off three Psychs with the last shots from his pistol, but three more of enormous size were kneeling over Angel's legs and torso like hyenas over a gazelle, ripping his flesh away with their teeth. Catfish punched, slashed, and stabbed at their backs, but they hardly paid him any notice. Several smaller Psychs, crowded out by the others, or perhaps just less aggressive, hung back like cubs waiting for their turn at the kill.

Sands and Catfish managed to pull one of the giants away, but Sands had to knife him three times in the base of the skull before he went down. They turned back to rejoin the attack, but they saw that Angel had quit struggling. His hands were free, and in each one he held a grenade. With a last look to his comrades, he pulled the pins.

Sands and Catfish ran and dove over a stack of bodies. The shockwave from the grenades hit them like a punch in the chest, and they could feel the shrapnel thudding against the wall of flesh that protected them. The blast tore a wide gash in the top of the Arena. Insulation from the ceiling above fell like a heavy snow.

In the Vestibule there was an uneasy, tearful silence. The screens all went blank with the blast. Oleg tapped futilely at the keys of his console, trying to locate a live feed. Ahmer turned down the master volume to squelch the angry roar of static. The others looked questioningly at one another. In the horror and confusion they had witnessed on screen, they were not even sure of what had happened.

"Was that an explosion?" someone asked.

"I think Angel had a grenade," said another.

"Did Sands and Catfish make it to cover?"

In the wayward beams of the few lights that still burned in the Arena, dust swirled, creating a yellow, hazy glow. The air was acrid with charred flesh and blood. Sands and Catfish struggled to their feet. The threat was over. The few Psychs who weren't dead they finished off with pistol shots or a knife to the brain. They found Angel, his face almost unblemished, his eyes half-closed, as if lapsing into slumber. The rest of him was a mass of mangled flesh and bone that Sands could not bear to look at. The glint of Angel's gold cross caught his eye. He knelt to retrieve it. The chain was broken, and the cross came away easily in his hand. Catfish knelt beside him and placed his hand on Sands' shoulder. Sands heard him mutter a prayer, but he didn't know what it was.

After a moment of profound stillness, the two men stood. Sands looked up, through the rip in the Arena's dome, at the balcony from where Einstein used to watch the Battles.

"Let's blow this fuckin' place."

He yanked two grenades from his belt, pulled the pins with his teeth. Catfish did the same. Sands silently counted three. They threw their grenades up into the balcony and ran for cover. With four thundering explosions,

Einstein's masterwork of scientific horrors was blown to bits.

-18-

One today is worth two tomorrows.
—Benjamin Franklin

Sands sat in a corner of the Vestibule, brooding over the gold crucifix in his palm. He stared at the tiny figure, at the head wreathed in thorns, at the almost featureless face. He went deep into his meditative state, blocking out all that was around him, focusing on the little point of beard, the nub of nose, the two indentations that served for eyes. He tried to conjure out of that tiny piece of sculpted metal a human face, but no image of a benevolent Savior would come. Somehow, he didn't even see Angel. Instead he saw the shining eyes of Rabbi Ben-Ezra—Bloodyface—and heard his lips whisper his final appeal: *Elohim!*

"Sands! Sands, snap out of it! We don't have time for this!"

Victoria stood over him, her hand poised. After twenty seconds of calling his name and getting no response, she was ready to slap him across the face.

"Huh? What is it?"

"We need you."

She pointed over to the command center, where the Drones were huddled in conference, throwing worried glances his way.

"You okay, Bro?"

He hadn't even noticed Catfish standing there.

"Yeah. Let's get to it."

He closed his hand over the crucifix and stuffed it in his pocket. The Drones got up to meet him halfway, but he waved them back to their seats and joined them at their consoles. Oleg stood to make his report.

"We've got some systems back online, but we can't kill the engines and we can't change course. If we'd taken over the lab instead of blowing it up—"

Sands silenced him with a look.

"Just sayin'."

"But there is manual override," Ahmer said. "If we get to the engine room we can turn the rudder. We can even shut down the engines."

Bao shook his head. "None of that matters if we don't defuse that bomb."

Sands sighed. "We lost our bomb expert when we lost Wolf."

There was a sound of defeat in Sands' voice that Victoria had never heard before. She looked at Catfish. He had caught it, too.

"You can defuse that bomb," Catfish declared. "You've done it before."

"It's been a long time, man."

"So? I hear it's just like riding a bicycle."

Sands waited him out. Catfish threw his hands in the air.

"Okay, an exploding bicycle. But it's the same principle."

"You saw that rig. I'd probably just blow us all up."

"You think you've lost your touch?"

"What touch?"

Catfish's voice rose with irritation. "The touch in your ten fingers. Which you still all have, by the way."

Sands looked back at him, his expression inscrutable. "Maybe you think it's something else I got blown off."

"Well, why don't you *show* me."

Staring Catfish right in the face, Sands reached deep into his pants. The Drones, en masse, took half a step back. Sands pulled out his hand—middle finger extended. The two men laughed.

Victoria caught a look from Lani, and they shared a single thought: *Men.*

"All right," Sands said, the edge of command back in his voice. "How do we get down there?"

"The elevators are still dead," Oleg replied. "But at least the stairways are clear."

"Except for the ten thousand maniacs on the loose," Catfish grumbled.

"Actually, I calculate it is only about three thousand," Hari clarified.

Catfish rolled his eyes in Hari's direction. "That makes me feel so much better."

Ahmer cut in. "We could guide you to the engine room from here. But it might be better if one of us went with you."

Sands asked, "Are you volunteering?"

Ahmer swallowed and forced a nod.

"Say it."

"Yes, I am volunteering."

"Hari, what about you?"

"Yes, please!"

Sands clapped him on the shoulder. "Good man."

"Hey," Catfish cut in. "What am I, the B team?"

Sands took an apple from a basket of fruit and held it up to Ahmer. "Any more of this?"

"In the galley."

"And stores," Lani added. "There's tons of it."

Sands tossed the apple to Catfish. "We need allies. There're people on this ship that'll sell their souls for one of those."

Catfish turned the apple over in his hand and passed it to Victoria. "Said Eve to the Serpent."

***

Sands led Ahmer and Hari down the main stairwell, which stretched above and below them like the dark interior of a vast chimney. He wanted to double-time it down the steel stairs but was frustrated by the slow pace of the two young men, who moved clumsily under the burden of their equipment and shoulder-slung guns.

They came to the landing marked **4 GREED 4**. Ahmer consulted his tablet.

"These stairs lead all the way to the hold. But we should not go farther past Deck Six."

"Why's that?"

Ahmer seemed to want to pause on the steps to continue the conversation, but Sands kept moving down towards the next level.

"I think we should like to avoid lower decks. Better to take the maintenance shaft."

"Good idea. We need to pick up the pace, though. Let's move it, Hari!"

"Coming, Mr. Sands!"

There was a cry of surprise from above and the clatter of metal on metal as Hari's rifle came tumbling down at Sands' feet.

Hari almost went over the rail trying to catch up to his gun. Sands snatched it up from the steps and shoved it into Hari's chest. "Let's try not to kill ourselves before the Psychs get the chance."

"Yes, Mr. Sands. Sorry, Mr. Sands."

Sands looked down at Hari's neon-bright high-tops, the laces a spaghetti-like tangle.

"And lace up those shoes!"

"Yes, sir. I'll catch up."

Hari knelt down to tie his laces as the other two continued down. Sands moved quickly, wishing he could leave Hari and Ahmer both behind. Hari considered just giving the laces a yank, wrapping the excess around his ankles and tying a knot, but it would be sloppy, and he didn't think Sands would like it. He began methodically threading the laces though each eyehole, his concentration such that he didn't notice the face watching him from a crack in the Deck Four hatch.

***

Catfish burst into the galley stores with weapon drawn and made a quick sweep of the area. "Clear!"

Victoria, Bao, and Lani entered behind him. They stood on a raised platform that looked out on pallets and pallets of food. Catfish froze to the spot, taking in the spectacle with awe.

"Is that all...food?"

"Just like mom used to—" The unfortunately phrased quip died on Bao's lips at the sight of Catfish's pained expression. "I mean—you know what I mean. Like real food. Like you used to get before..."

"Yeah, kid. I know." He smiled. "Race you down."

Catfish bounded down the steps past Victoria and Lani like a little kid in a race for the ice cream truck. The first crate he came to was full of yellow onions. He grabbed one and held it up to his nose, rapturously sniffing it like a rose. He noticed the crate next to it. "Peppers!" He took one in his hands and bit into it like an apple. "Oh, my. We gonna cook up a mess o' gumbo tonight!"

Victoria, who had not gone so long without fresh food as Catfish, surveyed the crates and pallets with a more calculating eye. "It's a lot of food, all right. But it's a big ship. How long will it last?"

Bao consulted with Lani over his tablet. "Four weeks supply of fresh in cold storage. If you factor in frozen and non-perishables, maybe six months' worth."

Lani pointed out something to Bao on his tablet. "Those numbers are just for guards and crew, though."

"Well, we don't have to worry about them anymore. How long for everybody on the ship now? Us and all the inmates?"

Bao shrugged, did a quick calculation. "Thirty, forty days, maybe." He cut a glance at Catfish, who was eyes-deep in a mango. "That is, if people don't get carried away."

"I heard that."

Catfish tossed aside the pit of his mango and licked the juice from his fingers. "What's that rumbling noise? The engines?"

Bao shot a look at Lani. "I'll show you."

He led them to a hatch mounted in the floor like an entrance to a storm cellar. When he opened it, the rumble grew immediately louder, and there was an updraft of air that smelled of seawater with an overlay of something sweet and rank. Catfish looked down a flight of metal stairs, sniffing the air skeptically.

"What is it?"

"It's where they make Process."

Bao led them down to a platform that overlooked a massive rush of water gushing through a sieve the size of a panel truck. The sieve fed into a giant vat with sluices and pipes leading in and out from all directions. Bao had to shout over the noise.

"Every prison ship has its own self-contained plant."

"Is that seawater?" Catfish asked.

"That's right. The sieve works just like the baleen of a humpback whale. As the water passes through, it filters out the seaweed, plankton, all the organic matter."

"And that's what Process is made of?" Catfish was pleasantly surprised. "That doesn't sound so bad."

"ALL the organic matter," Victoria reiterated. She turned to the two Drones. "And not just from seawater, right?"

Bao and Lani exchanged an uncomfortable look.

"Show us."

They descended to the plant floor. Consulting his tablet again, Bao led them to a large, enclosed sluice that was fed by many pipes. He found a hinged metal lid, pausing before he opened it as if he hoped someone would stop him. He took hold of the handle and lifted the lid wide, letting it clang on its hinges as he stepped back. Everyone else held their noses against the stench as they gaped down at a metal screw that churned through a thick brown glop. Victoria looked at Catfish with the perverse satisfaction of one who knows how the sausage is made.

"Potato peels, toenail clippings, food wrappers, engine oil—anything carbon-based and everything flushed down the toilet..."

Catfish blanched.

Victoria hefted the lid and banged it shut. "It's the circle of life, baby."

"Now you see why we don't eat it," Lani said. "Plus, there's the drugs they put in it."

"Here's something I'm betting you don't know," Victoria said. "Parolees and the dead are negative assets on this ship—but they have something very valuable."

As if he had already guessed, Catfish said, "Their organs."

"Gold star for you. Organs, bone marrow, stem cells—it all gets harvested and shipped to clearing houses, where the bits and pieces are auctioned off to the highest bidders. What's left over, well..." She shrugged and patted the lid on the sluice.

The others looked sick.

"Gives new meaning to the old saying, doesn't it? Waste not, want not."

***

Sands held up a hand to signal halt as he and Ahmer came to the landing marked **6 HERESY 6**. He gazed at the legend and snorted in recognition.

"Six letters. First time I ever noticed."

Ahmer looked at him quizzically.

"Six letters in the word 'heresy.' Six-six-six. Some joke."

Ahmer didn't get it.

"It's a Christian thing."

Sands peered through the glass porthole in the closed hatch. All clear. He put his hand to the latch to lead on, but he realized Hari wasn't with them.

"Where's Hari?"

Ahmer looked back. "Right behind. I heard his footsteps. I think."

Sands listened. "Well, there's no footsteps now. He didn't turn off at the wrong deck, did he?"

They stepped back to get a good look up the stairwell. Nothing.

"Hari!" Sands' voice reverberated off the hard metal surfaces that surrounded them. It was answered by a scream.

Sands leapt to the stairs, taking them three at a time. Ahmer scrambled after him.

Another scream.

"Hari, hold on!" Ahmer shouted.

Sands looked up just in time to see Hari come over the rail. He flew out, as if he had leapt—or been pitched—and sailed across the rectangle of empty space, landing at the base of the steps on the other side. Sands heard the bone-crushing impact below, but he kept his eyes upward. When a ghoulish face looked over the rail he was ready. He squeezed off a burst from his bullpup, and the Psych went tumbling down the well until he was nothing but a dull thump in the darkness.

Sands scrambled back down the steps to where Hari had landed. Ahmer was already there, Hari's broken body cradled in his arms. His eyes were open, but his breath was strained, his mouth and nostrils running with blood.

Sands bent down and pressed a hand to his narrow shoulder. He wanted to tell him it would be all right, but he knew it wouldn't.

Hari struggled to speak. "Sorry...Mr. Sands..."

His last breath rattled to silence. Ahmer turned shining eyes to Sands, but if he wanted some word or gesture of comfort, Sands had none for him. Instead, he grimaced in rage and grabbed Ahmer by the shoulders.

"You stick with me—do you hear? Do you hear!" He shook Ahmer into a violent nod of assent. "From now on, we're joined at the fucking *hip!*"

He shoved Ahmer back to the deck, his eyes blazing, but there was something in them besides anger. He turned away, his head down, standing with his back to Ahmer as if taking a moment to gather his strength. Ahmer watched as Sands straightened his massive shoulders, took three steps toward the Deck Six hatch, and stopped. Ahmer got to his feet. Sands still waited, his hand on the latch. He didn't open it until Ahmer fell into step behind him.

-19-

All sorrows are bearable, if there is bread.

—Cervantes

On Gluttony Deck, Catfish strolled down the rows of cells behind a pushcart laden with fruit, singing out like a New Orleans street vendor.

"Fresh fr-u-u-u-it! Red ap-ples! Juicy pea-ches! Ripe ba-na-na-a-a-s! Fresh fru-u-u-it!"

In Catfish's imagination he was tossing the fruit out to eagerly waiting hands, the way he had seen generous vendors do back home with hungry street kids, but the illusion was spoiled by the narrow grates that many inmates could not even get four fingers through. He could slip the bananas and peaches through easily enough, but the apples had to be cut in two with his knife. It slowed him down, but the inmates were grateful and full of questions.

"Hey man," one called, as he sucked on a peach pit. "What happened to the treadmills? They ain't come on since yesterday."

"Why, you miss 'em?"

The man looked down at his belly. He still had an ample paunch, but his pants were so loose he had to hold them up with one hand.

"Not much. You turned 'em off?"

"We sure did." In truth, the treadmills hadn't operated since the ship had gone to emergency power, but Catfish saw no harm in the lie.

"Who's 'we'?"

"We, the motherfuckin' people, my friend. You'll be joining us pretty soon."

The man nodded his thanks, too happy to speak.

"Hey! Hey, fruit man!" The man in the next cell must have been a recent transfer to the block. He still had what the guards called "baby fat." In other words, his skin was still tight. He hadn't yet suffered the catastrophic weight loss that left so many denizens of Gluttony Deck with sagging folds of loose skin.

"Ap-ples, pea-ches, ba-na-nas—what'll ya have?"

"You got any donuts?"

Catfish gave him the eye as he pushed a peach through the grate. The man caught it and gave it a glum look. But the aroma caught him by surprise. He smiled and sank his teeth into the fruit, the juice running over his lips.

On Lust Deck, Victoria and Lani carried large trays from which they doled out sliced meats, fruits, and cheeses. A huge clamor rose up as word of the food spread throughout the block, but the two women maintained their composure, pausing at each cell as if they were passing out hors d'oeuvres at some posh gala.

One woman asked if they were going to be released. "Soon," Lani told her. "You got to detoxify first. The Process you've been eating is full of drugs."

The woman nodded her understanding. "When?"

Lani involuntarily glanced at her watch. Never, she thought, if Sands can't defuse the bomb. "Tomorrow," she said. "Maybe the next day."

Victoria came to the cell of an old woman with wide, sunken eyes. She had to be coaxed to the grate to get her portion, Victoria beckoning her with a piece of hard cheese the size of two fingers.

"What is it?"

"It's cheese."

She pressed it into the woman's outstretched hand, which was thin enough to fit through the grate.

"Process cheese?"

"No, honey. Real cheese. From a cow."

The woman sniffed at it, pulled back at the sharp smell. But then she sniffed it again and nibbled a corner. Tears welled up in her eyes.

"Here," Victoria offered. "Take some more."

The old woman shook her head. She held the morsel in her two hands like a priest praying over the Host. "Make sure everyone gets some."

Victoria swallowed against a lump that rose in her throat. "I will."

On Limbo Deck, where the inmates were so clean and well-fed they could have been tourists on some sort of bizarre fantasy cruise, Bao and Desmond did not fare so well as the others. The normally docile Limboers knew by their internal clocks that their midday ration of Process was fourteen minutes late, and they were not about to accept any substitute. The fruits and vegetables they had been given they flung back through the slots in their cell grates, some with enough force and accuracy to pelt Bao and Desmond as they retreated from the block.

"We want Process!" they chanted, rattling their cages like enraged apes. "We want Process!"

"What the hell!" Bao cried, as a carrot speared him in the side of the head.

"We-want-Pro-cess!! We-want-Pro-cess!!"

A peach hurtled at Desmond's feet. He stepped on it, spilling his basket of fruit as his foot went sideways. He got to one knee to try to gather up what he had dropped, when someone above began spitting out mouthfuls of masticated banana.

"Let's get out of here!" Bao shouted. Desmond didn't argue.

***

Sands and Ahmer were at the lowest deck of the ship, making their way to the Engine Room. They were in some sort of hold where engine parts, machinery, and equipment were stored, much of it rusted and ready for scrap. The hold was dank, the bulkheads cold and wet as the walls of a limestone cave. Dripping water and the scuttling sound of what Sands hoped were mere rats echoed all around them. Ahmer was stumbling and near-blind in the darkness, but Sands felt like he could really see for the first time in days. After three years living in the gloom of Treachery Deck, the shadowy twilight of the hold was a welcome relief to his weakened eyes.

The scrape of a footstep alerted Sands that something other than a rat was stalking them. Ahmer, who was so on edge that he jumped at every sound he heard, didn't even notice the footfall, unable to distinguish it from the white noise of imagined threats around him.

Sands shifted his bullpup to his right hand, locking the shoulder strap around his elbow. With his right he unsheathed his knife and held the blade ready against his thigh. He didn't yet know the nature of their stalker. Was it another of those beasts that had killed Wolf? Was it a Psych? Or was it a man—some stranded hand, or even an inmate who had somehow managed to escape his cell? It could even be Einstein.

Ahmer hadn't heard the sound, but he noticed the change in Sands' demeanor.

"What is it?"

Sands held a finger to his lips. The sight of the big knife in his hand made Ahmer's eyes go wide.

In that moment of distraction, a Psych leapt out of the shadows. He came from Sands' blind side, but he spoiled his advantage with a wild screech that gave Sands the moment he needed to meet the charge with a broad-arm to the chest. Sands drove his knife blade through the Psych's throat to his spine. The hulk crumpled to the deck, his arms and legs gone limp. Sands didn't strike another blow. He just watched until he was sure the last bit of life had drained away.

Staring up at him, the face looked much like that of any other Psych Sands had seen. Like Bloodyface, the man's visage was altered not just by insanity, but physically distorted by whatever chemical processes had driven him mad. It concerned Sands that he was so far below decks. It meant the Psychs could be spread all throughout the ship.

Sands wiped the blood from his knife on the Psych's pants and turned to Ahmer. The young Pakistani wobbled on unsteady legs, his mouth open and eyes glassy, like a person on the verge of a faint. But they had no time for that.

"How much farther?"

The question brought Ahmer out of his funk, giving him something else to focus on besides his fear. He stared at his tablet as if trying to make it out through a thick fog.

"Just ahead."

"Lead the way."

Before Ahmer could protest or even hesitate, Sands pushed him forward. After a few twists and turns around decaying machinery and stacks of pallets, they came to a large vault-like hatch in the bulkhead.

"This is it?"

"Yes. The Engine Room is through here."

Sands tried the wheel-lock, but the hatch wouldn't budge. "Can you unseal it?"

Ahmer checked his controls. "No. Someone used manual override to seal it from the other side."

Sands ran his hands and eyes over the hatch, exploring it for weaknesses. The hinges were as big as his arms. He took hold of the Wheelock again and strained with everything he had.

"I think it moved! Help me!"

Ahmer doubted it had moved. Next to Sands' meaty hooks he placed his own hands, looking like an underfed baby's by comparison. He pulled as hard as he could, even as he thought how ludicrous it was to imagine his meager strength could make any difference against bolts of heavy tempered steel.

Sands released the Wheelock, gasping with spent effort, his face red.

"Shit! Shit!"

He pulled two grenades from his belt, the only two he had. "Maybe we can blow it."

He fumbled about at the hinges, looking for some way he could effectively place the grenades.

Ahmer shook his head. "The door is too strong, Sands."

"We just need more firepower. We can go back to the weapons cache and get some C-4."

"There is no time."

Sands checked his watch: Twenty-three minutes... Twenty-two-fifty-nine...fifty-eight....

"Goddammit!"

Sands' breath labored like a bull's. He cast about with starting eyes—looking, thinking, looking—until he fixed on something. On the adjacent bulkhead, high above a stack of drums, was the emblem of the 600-Cell, and below it, just legible through layers of grime, was the motto: *In hoc signo vinces.*

Seeing the look in Sands' eyes, Ahmer stepped back, fearing his friend had gone mad. Sands took his bullpup in his hands, and with a cry of rage let loose a spray of fire that sent cartridges pinging off the deck and bullets ricocheting through the hold like blind hornets.

Ahmer clapped his hands to his ears and screamed, "Sands! Stop shooting! Sands, *stop!*"

The gun went quiet and Sands fell to his knees. He banged the butt of his rifle on the deck.

"Why! Why can't one motherfuckin' thing go right!"

Breathing heavily, he looked at his rifle like he meant to fling it across the hold, but instead he lay it on the deck. He sat back on his haunches, his head bowed in thought, but canting back and forth in despair of finding any answers.

Ahmer realized Sands had not gone mad, but he had never seen him at such a loss. He tried to think of some words of encouragement—but what words could one such as he say to a man like Sands that would not be laughed at? "Sands," he began—but something caught his eye.

One of Sands' errant shots had pierced an oil drum, and the oil that leaked from it had begun to puddle on the deck. Ahmer watched as the puddle sent out a tendril that meandered its way to a groove in the center of the deck and then down to a round, iron grate. Ahmer checked his tablet, scrolling through schematics until he found the one that showed where that drain might go.

Yes. That was it.

"Sands! Sands, look—the drain!"

Sands looked. He watched as Ahmer bent over the drain and laced his fingers through the grate and lifted.

"It's not even bolted!"

Ahmer tugged at it. It was heavy as a manhole cover, held in place only by its own weight.

In an instant, Sands was there, and together they lifted the drain cover away and eased it to the deck with a dull clang. Sands peered inside, but all he could see was darkness.

"Where does it go?"

"It's a—" Ahmer consulted his tablet and hesitated over the strange word. "A *bil-jah* drain..."

"Bilge," Sands said. "A bilge drain."

"Yes. The bilge compartment runs under this whole deck. There's another drain in the Engine Room."

"Got it."

Sands dropped down, trying to squeeze through, but he couldn't get past his knees. He tried both legs, then one at time, and even seemed ready to plunge through head first, but the opening was just too small.

After watching several fruitless contortions, Ahmer tapped Sands on the shoulder.

"I can do it."

He scooted forward, dropped his legs through with room to spare. Sands gripped his shoulder.

"You're going nowhere without me."

"No time to argue. It's not far. I can do it."

Sands realized it was pointless to say anything more.

Ahmer handed Sands his tablet. "Take good care of that."

Sands nodded.

Ahmer shimmied his hips through and sank down to his armpits. Sands took him by the hand, pumped it once for good luck. Ahmer flushed, looking sheepish.

"All those years going hungry in Pakistan," he said. "They finally pay off."

Sands blinked at him. "Did you just crack wise?"

Ahmer answered with a weak smile and lowered himself down.

There was a yelp, a splash, and what sounded to Sands' ears like cursing in Urdu. He couldn't see anything.

"Ahmer, are you okay?"

Ahmer's torch came on and waved back and forth. "Okay. See you on the other side."

"The other side, Brother. Be careful."

Ahmer wasn't sure at first he had heard right. "Brother" was what Sands called Catfish. It was what he called Angel and Wolf before they were killed. It was a word for brave soldiers. His heart danced in his chest. He wanted to shout for joy. But he thought perhaps this wasn't the appropriate time.

He moved forward, slogging through rancid, oily water that was knee deep. The bilge compartment was shallow, no more than six or seven feet in depth, but it was as wide and as long as the ship's hull, the expanse broken only with the steel buttresses that formed the ship's skeleton. The place was alive with rats. They scuttled up and down the walls through the roving beam of Ahmer's flash. He kept it moving, in hopes of warding off any creatures that might venture too close. Except for his feeble beam, he could make out nothing but endless darkness. Only by keeping his movement perpendicular to the buttresses could he be sure he was moving in the right direction. He stumbled repeatedly, going to his knees several times, the turgid bilge sloshing up to his waist. Behind him a low, rhythmic moaning—perhaps an animal, perhaps the straining joints of the ship—kept him moving forward.

In the Engine Room, the noise of Sands' gunfire had attracted Cerberus to the other side of the hatch. Six separate nostrils sniffed at the seal, but it found nothing but the familiar scent of its master, where he had passed through a short time before. Limping slightly from a wound on one of its forelegs, Cerberus moved to the bilge drain. One mastiff head sniffed as the other two heads cocked their ears to listen. Nothing there. The creature moved on, continuing its watchful rounds.

-20-

We must do the things we think we cannot do.

—Eleanor Roosevelt

Oleg, alone in the Vestibule, sat at his console, brooding over an on-screen document with the heading "EMERGENCY PROTOCOLS." It was a sobering document that detailed many catastrophic scenarios, but thematically speaking, it all boiled down to this: "Officers and VIPs first, save whatever part of the crew you can, let the inmates go down with the ship." He learned at least that the self-destruct mechanism in the *Inferno*'s bowels was not just some jerry-rigged improvisation, but that it was a design feature of every black raft. There had to be some protocol for disengaging it, he thought. Or at least, some clue how he might escape it.

His screen glitched and went staticky. He tried to scroll to the next page of the document, but the screen glitched again. He cursed and slapped the console on the side, a technique that never worked but always made him feel better. The screen went to complete snow. He cursed again, and was about to give it a good whack, when he noticed that there was something moving in the snow. An image, like the outline of a head. The outline clarified, and a face emerged. It was Einstein.

Oleg glanced around to check whether anyone else had seen it. But the old man was asleep and the others were all away on their silly mission of mercy to feed the Dregs. He peered at Einstein's face with fascination. The strange-looking man fiddled off-camera at some controls, seemingly unaware that anyone might be watching him.

The glitchiness subsided, and Einstein leaned forward, looking Oleg almost directly in the eye. Oleg checked the black electrical tape over his monitor's camera. It was still secure. Instead of looking at what was probably a blank screen, Einstein was looking into his own terminal's camera, giving the illusion of eye contact. He began to speak, his voice coming in over Oleg's speakers at a low, conspiratorial pitch.

"This is Dr. Garrick Henderson calling the operator of Terminal One in the Vestibule. Do you read?"

Oleg sputtered into his microphone, "Y-yes."

"This is Dr. Garrick Henderson—"

Oleg realized his microphone was unplugged. He jacked it in.

"Yes, this is Terminal One," he said.

"Good. Please remove the obstruction from your terminal camera."

Oleg peeled away the tape. Einstein smiled.

"That's better." Einstein consulted a clipboard. "Is this Technical Operator IN-47632, Oleg Kral?"

"Yes."

"Are you alone?"

"Yes. Everyone else is below decks."

Einstein grunted. "Thank you for that bit of information. Since your friends destroyed my laboratory's surveillance system I am all but blind." Einstein detected something in Oleg's expression. "They are your friends?"

"They're no friends of mine."

"I see. Well, Oleg—may I call you Oleg? The reason I'm calling is that this ship is about to self-destruct in..." He checked his watch. "Eighteen minutes. I'm in the Warden's escape pod—"

Oleg had a question, but Einstein cut him off. "I know—it's a secret. Just like the chute from his quarters to the pod is a secret. Except now you know the secret, too. Anyhoo, it appears the Warden was concerned someone, say, in an emergency situation, might steal his pod out from under him, and so he's hidden its command module. Without which, I'm sure you can guess, the pod will not go."

Einstein adjusted his camera to show an angle on the pod's control panel. There was an empty slot. "It fits here. It would be about the size of a pack of cards." The camera shifted back to Einstein's face. "Without that module, I'm stuck. And the Warden's escape chute isn't a two-way conveyance. One may ride it down, but one may not ride it back up. So you see, I can't retrieve the module myself."

"I could get it for you."

"You read my mind. You'll find the module in the Warden's quarters. If you can bring it to me within—" He checked his watch again. "Sixteen-and-a-half minutes, well—the pod will easily accommodate two."

Before Oleg could answer, Bao and Desmond burst in, brushing the last of the vegetable debris from their clothes. On Oleg's screen, Einstein blinked out.

"Man, it's crazy!" Bao was saying. "Hey, Oleg, I think those freaks on Limbo Deck are addicted to Process."

Oleg discreetly placed the tape back over his terminal camera.

"I'm sure they would have killed us had they gotten the opportunity," Desmond added. "They wanted no part of fruits and vegetables."

"Maybe you should try them with meat," Oleg offered.

"Sure, I bet if we fried up some bacon they'd change their tune."

Oleg's console speaker crackled to life.

"Oleg, this is Sands, come in."

Instead of answering, Oleg jumped to his feet. "You guys take over. I've got to hit the head." Before they could respond, he was gone.

To Desmond's questioning look Bao responded, "Too much dairy."

The speaker crackled again. "Oleg, this is Sands, do you read me?"

Bao sat at the console. "Sands, this is Bao, come in."

"Any word from Catfish on those reinforcements?"

"Last I heard, he's got a half-dozen men. They're in the magazine now, getting equipped."

"Okay, get him on the horn and tell him to bring some C-4 to the Engine Room. Anything he can find that blows up."

"Roger."

"Sands out."

***

Victoria and Lani exited the Lust Deck prison block, their trays empty but their spirits full of good feeling.

Lani, especially, was bubbling over with the emotional connections she had made with the women. She had never been to Lust Deck—or any of the prison decks—before, and it was the most women she had seen all at once in over a year.

"It's going to be so amazing when we can open the cells and let everybody out."

"It'll be amazing all right," Victoria agreed, but she was thinking there were plenty of *Inferno* inmates that were better left in their cells.

They came to a T-junction in the passageway. "Which way?"

Lani checked her tablet. She pointed at the bulkhead straight ahead, where there was a half-open hatch. "That looks like a shortcut."

"What is it?"

Lani read off the schematic. "Physical plant. Ventilation, plumbing, that kind of stuff. It goes straight to the mezzanine."

"Okay."

Victoria went first, pushing the hatch wide. The compartment looked something like a utility room, with tools and equipment stowed on one wall. The rest was a webwork of pipes, ducting, and conduit. The center of this tangle was a clear path, and although the space was dimly lit, Victoria could make out what looked like an ell turn not far ahead.

"Are you sure about this?"

Lani stepped through the hatch, her eyes on her tablet. "I think so. According to this, it should be a straight shot."

Victoria bent to take a look. The shattering clang of the hatch slamming shut behind them caused both women to gasp in fright. Their trays clattered to the deck. If Lani's tablet hadn't been secured by a strap to her hip, she would have dropped it, too.

Standing at the hatch was a leering, bearded hulk. With one hand he spun the wheel-lock secure. In the other he swung a heavy chain, the end tangled into a ball to form a sort of mace.

"Well whatta ya know. Here I am going to Lust Deck, and it looks like Lust Deck has come to me."

The hulk looked to be more beast than man. His beard was short, but thick and wiry as steel wool, and all of a piece with the hair on his head. The bristles grew so high on his cheeks as to almost form a mask. They carpeted his neck and peeked out in tufts from the holes in his filthy smock. What was visible of his face was pockmarked and red, like many of the Psychs, but his eyes were frighteningly sane. He smiled with blackened teeth and loomed toward them, jangling the ball at the end of his chain.

As one, the women picked up their trays, flung them at him, and ran. He batted the trays away with a sweep of one forearm and hurled his mace with the other. The chain caught Lani in the legs, the ball whipping around and thudding in the small of her back. She hit the deck hard.

Victoria skidded to a halt at Lani's cry. She stooped and grabbed her under one arm to pull her up, but Lani's legs were tangled in the chain. Before she could kick it away, the hulk had her by the ankle. Lani looked Victoria in the eye and gritted out one word: "Run!"

Victoria released Lani' arm, but instead of running she tried to make a play for a pry-bar on the wall. The hulk yanked the chain from Lani's legs, causing her to cry out in pain as the heavy iron links raked across her bones. Victoria pulled at the pry-bar, but like all things onboard a ship, it was secured. A second tug pulled it away, but the hulk swung the ball of his chain down on the bar with such force that it rattled Victoria's teeth. If it had hit her, it would have broken her arm.

She ran. The hulk whipped the chain in an arc around his head and let it fly, but Lani spoiled his aim with a kick to his knee. The blow jarred her, like she had kicked a lamppost. The lamppost growled and kicked back.

Victoria quickly found that the "ell" she thought she had seen was a dead end. A series of widely spaced pipes confronted her like the bars of a cell. Instead of a passageway, they had stumbled into a closed compartment. Surprised to find the pry-bar still in her hand, she banged it against the pipes, but even if she could have bent or broken them, it would have been to no purpose. Beyond the pipes was nothing but bare wall. She looked up. A single, dimly burning bulb stared down at her. She swung the pry-bar at it, plunging the area into darkness.

The hulk followed after her, holding Lani by one foot, her body slung over his shoulder like a rucksack. She tried her best to kick him in the head, but he only batted her foot away like a pesky fly. "Whatsa matter, Red? Don't you wanna party?"

Coming to the dead end, he dropped Lani like a sack of potatoes and pinned her with one foot on her neck. Every time she struggled, he only had to shift his weight to make her still. He cast about to see where Victoria could be hiding, but she was invisible in the shadows.

"I'm giving you ten seconds to come out, Red, or things might get ugly." He looked down at Lani, her face red with the pressure he was applying. "You know, I don't get too hung up on a woman's looks. Or if she's breathin'."

Squeezing between the narrow space between the pipes and the bulkhead, Victoria cursed herself for having agreed to Lani's suggestion they leave their heavy weapons behind. They had been on a mission of mercy and they didn't want to spook the vulnerable women of Lust Deck with assault rifles. Idiot! And where was her pistol? She felt for her holster, but it was empty. The gun must have been knocked loose in the scuffle. All she could do now was maneuver to outflank her adversary and hope to gain an advantage. If she moved carefully, the hum of machinery was enough to cover the sound of her movements. It was slow going, but already she was parallel to his shoulder.

"Come on out and play, Red. I'm plenty of man for two."

"You stay right where you are, Victoria!"

The hulk lifted his foot and jabbed Lani in the temple with his heel, bouncing her head off the deck.

"See? We're havin' fun already!"

Victoria spotted a way to climb up to the ductwork overhead. She called out, "Lani, are you all right?"

"I'm fine," Lani grunted, her face pressed again to the deck by the hulk's foot. Her voice betrayed more anger than fear.

The hulk spun to follow the sound of Victoria's voice, but she had already ducked behind a panel, where she was able to move more freely. She clambered up the pipes to the ceiling.

The hulk pulled Lani up by the hair and circled one arm around her neck. With one forearm hooked under her chin, he held her with her legs dangling. She kicked and punched at him, but it was like hitting a refrigerator. Rattling his chain across the deck, the hulk made his way to where he thought Victoria was hiding. As he moved forward, Victoria, from her perch overhead, maneuvered around to his blind side.

Displaying Lani like an oversized doll, he scraped the steel brush of his beard against her cheek.

"She's a cute little thing, ain't she? How'd you think she'd look with her head on backwards?"

He tightened his arm around her neck. Lani's small hands pulled and scratched. Her legs kicked.

Victoria was directly above them now.

Lani had gone limp. The hulk eased his grip and slapped her cheek.

"Wakey-wakey. You don't wanna miss the fun."

Lani struggled back to consciousness, her fingers squeezing in between her neck and her attacker's arm, desperate to make any space for breath she could get.

The hulk shouted into the darkness. "You wanna watch, is that it? You kinky bitch. Okay, watch this."

He looped his chain around Lani's neck. Lani grimaced in pain.

"What ya wanna bet I can pop her head like a pimple?"

Victoria leapt from her perch, bringing the pry-bar down on his head with a bone-splitting crack.

The hulk fell onto his back, both hands gripping his bleeding head. Victoria pounced on him, shoving the pry-bar into his throat, pressing it down on one end with both hands, on the other with her knee.

The hulk gagged, his hairy face gone purple. He grabbed the pry-bar, and Victoria could feel his tremendous strength. But before he could throw her off, Lani had picked up his mace, and swinging with all she had, brought the ball of chain squarely into his groin. The hulk let out a strangled squeak from somewhere deep in his throat. Lani hit him again and again, until his pants colored with blood.

The hulk squirmed and rocked, but the fight had gone out of him. Victoria sat on his chest, one knee on each shoulder. "What's the matter, big boy? Can't get it up when the woman's on top?"

He grimaced, and Lani saw the sinews of one great arm contract as he balled his fist for a blow. But before she could shout a warning, Victoria had jammed a knife into his throat. A geyser of blood shot out from his severed jugular and sprayed the bulkhead. Victoria backed off of him, coolly wiping the blood from her blade. The hulk clutched at his throat and kicked his legs, but his movements were feeble and sloth-like. With a final pulse of gore into the growing pool around his body, he went still.

"Victoria." Lani's voice was raspy and small. "You killed him."

Victoria sheathed her knife. "Believe me, that's the least of what he had planned for us."

-21-

I like a good hater.

—Samuel Johnson

Oleg didn't bother to avoid surveillance as he raced to the Warden's quarters. He hoped Bao and Desmond would be too preoccupied to notice as he ran by one camera after another, but even if they did see him, what could they do about it? They wouldn't leave the Vestibule unmanned, and everyone else was below decks. If what Einstein had told him about the Warden's escape contingencies was true, he would be in the Engine Room and on his way to freedom before they knew what was happening.

He burst into the Warden's quarters, heart and mind racing, but with no idea where to begin his search. The quarters weren't large—two rooms, the size of a small hotel suite—but they were cluttered, and like all ship's quarters, chock full of drawers, cupboards, and storage bins. He ignored the dinette, going straight to the main living area. He spent a full minute rifling drawers—small spaces where a small thing might be stashed—but he realized he was on the wrong track. In an emergency, one wants everything one needs in a single, easily accessible place. And it should be an obvious place. The Warden didn't strike Oleg as the kind of person who would bet his life on remembering exactly in which drawer he had stowed which thing way back when.

By the Warden's bunk—really an ample bed, Oleg noticed, with a luxurious overstuffed mattress—were two closets. He opened the first. In it was a clear acrylic capsule, just large enough for one person—even a plus-sized person like the Warden. So this was the escape chute. He saw the red button marked "Launch," next to warnings that read "Fasten Harness" and "Keep Hands Clear," but there was nothing else. He tried the next closet. It was full of what one would expect—shirts and pants on hangers, belts and ties on hooks—but at the bottom was a go-pack. And next to that was something that made Oleg's heart sink—a safe.

It was a standard hotel model—a twelve-key touchpad next to a four-digit readout. In normal circumstances, such low-grade security would have made Oleg laugh, but he had run out of the Vestibule without his tablet—and even if he'd had it, he didn't have the five minutes it would take to crack the thing.

What he needed was the combination. He keyed in on the go-pack. The zippered pockets were likely places, but he found them all empty except for useless junk like ballpoint pens and toenail clippers. He ripped open the main compartment and dumped out the contents—candy bars, two pints of booze, a wad of cash, and a handgun. Those few items seemed to sum up everything Oleg knew about the Warden. He stuffed the cash in his shirt and the weapon in his belt. There was comfort in having them, but they would be useless unless he could open that safe. He glanced at his watch—then looked again in disbelief. Could he have possibly used up that much time?

He fell to his knees before the safe. It was a gesture that mimicked his despair. Nothing left to do now but try hacking it the old-fashioned way. He stared at the touchpad, trying to put himself in the mind of the Warden. Nothing. Nothing. Nothing. Then, like an impulse from the reptile brain, hacker reflex kicked in. He keyed in 1-2-3-4.

The lock clicked.

"You gotta be—" A stream of hacker scorn piled up like boxcars at the back of his tongue, but he had no time for that. He opened the lid. There was the module. As he cradled it in his hands he was surprised to be looking at it through welling eyes. He felt something he hadn't felt in a long time—long before that terrible day his parents had signed away his freedom for the empty promises of *Inferno*. For the first time since he had been a little boy in Slovenia—back when old Mother Albina had awarded him a medal of St. Methodius for his recitation of the Nicene Creed—he felt the joy of one delivered by the grace of God.

He climbed into the capsule and strapped on the harness. It needed considerable tightening to fit him. He began tugging on the straps, when a sound like thunder shuddered through the ship. Oleg froze, fearing for a moment that he was too late, that the bomb had gone off. He checked his watch. It wasn't time. Eight minutes until detonation. Had something gone wrong? Had Einstein miscalculated? The explosion had been loud, but had it really come from within the ship? Had it sounded distant because it occurred somewhere off-ship, or had it merely been muffled because it occurred so far below decks? He stared at the red launch button. If he took the chute down to the Engine Room, would it mean escape, or would he be plunging into a flooded compartment with no way out? Oleg crossed himself, but if he had faith in anything, it was in technology and mathematical certainty. Cradling the module over his heart, he hit the launch button.

***

Lani and Victoria were Top-deck when the blast struck. A sound as sharp as a rifle shot sent them to their knees, followed by a deep rumble they felt in their guts. They clung to each other, their eyes wide, fearing to see or speak. But the ship did not pitch beneath them, and the rumble they heard seemed to come from far away. There was no fire or smoke, no warning from the ship's sirens.

"That wasn't the ship, was it?" Victoria's voice sounded like a frightened girl's in her ears. "I mean the bomb. That couldn't have been it."

"I don't think so."

They stood and scanned the ship. No damage was apparent. But over the foredeck they spotted a massive plume of black smoke thrusting up into the early morning sky. They ran to the rail to have a look.

Lani clapped her hand over her mouth. "Oh, my God!"

Stretching off toward the horizon were five more black rafts, churning northward in perfect formation. The nearest was in flames, spilling angry clouds into the sky and burning oil into the sea.

They ran to the Vestibule to find Bao, Desmond, and Rashid standing dumbstruck before the monitors. No one spoke. They all knew what it meant.

Sands' voice came crackling over the comm. "Bao, what was that?"

"The black rafts," Bao replied. "They're all converging. One of them just exploded."

As he spoke, the monitors crackled with the force of another explosion as the burning black raft broke in two.

"It's going down," Bao said. The two halves of the gigantic ship slipped beneath the waves with shocking speed, leaving nothing but a roiling, burning oil slick. Bao and the others stared at the image on the screens as if at a premonition of their own deaths.

"Where's Catfish?" Sands demanded.

Desmond nudged Bao and pointed to one of the other monitors. Catfish and his men were having a hot time with a crush of rampaging inmates on Deck Nine. Some of the inmates had guns.

"Deck Nine," Bao said. "It looks like he's having trouble.

Sands cursed, and he cut the conversation without signing off. There was nothing else to be said.

***

In the bilge, Ahmer slipped his thin fingers through the grate in the Engine Room floor above him. Standing on one of the steel buttresses that formed the skeleton of the hull, he could get just enough leverage to push against the grate, but the footing was treacherous. He had fallen twice already into the slick muck trying to get into position.

Doubt seized him as he felt the weight of the heavy iron against his palms. Was it bolted down? But no, it couldn't be, he told himself. Why would it be different from the other grate? He shoved again, as hard as he could, and the grate shifted. So it wasn't bolted. But it was so heavy, how would he ever be able to lift it?

He had an idea. Instead of using his arms, he would use his legs. He bent his knees, crouching until his arms were straight, his elbows locked. His feet trembled on their narrow hold on the buttress, but somehow he was able to thrust himself upward. The grate lifted, and drawing on a strength he didn't know he possessed, he edged the heavy iron disk out of its seat. Once he had accomplished that, it was just a matter of patience and a few well timed shoves to get the thing clear of the opening.

Ahmer's arms and legs were wobbly from the effort he had expended, his hands slick with bilge water and sweat, but he would not be denied now. He pulled himself up and gained the deck, gulping down the diesel-scented air of the Engine Room like sweet perfume. He hurried to the hatch, spun the wheel-lock, and pulled it wide.

Sands looked so happy to see Ahmer at the hatch he thought for a moment the big man would embrace him, but the look of joy on Sands' face quickly turned to disgust. Sands threw a hand over his nose and backed away, keeping his distance as he edged sidewise into the Engine Room. Ahmer looked at himself. He was covered from shoulders to shoes in greasy black muck.

"The bilge is a filthy place," he said.

Sands suppressed a gag and held out Ahmer's tablet. "Which way?"

It grieved Ahmer to touch an electronic device when he was so dirty, but he took it, trying not to be distracted by the black smudges that multiplied across the interface as he worked it. After a moment, he pointed. "That way."

At the far end of the compartment they came to another hatch. It was unsealed, but when Sands pushed against it there was resistance. Motioning Ahmer back, he readied his gun and shoved the hatch open with his foot. He stepped through, checked his perimeter, and gave Ahmer the all clear.

Ahmer stepped into the compartment. Nothing was amiss, as far as he could tell, but he was curious why the hatch had resisted opening. He pushed it back shut.

Ahmer's gasp spun Sands around. Strung up to the back of the hatch was Oleg, a wire around his neck, his eyes and tongue bulging. At his feet were his handgun and a smattering of loose cash. Ahmer stood transfixed at the sight of his murdered compatriot, but Sands only became more alert. Hunched over his bullpup, he swept and re-swept his eyes over the compartment, searching out any threat.

"What the hell is he doing here?" he growled over his shoulder.

Ahmer pointed out the pallet of C-4, just a few steps away.

"He must have come to try to defuse the bomb."

Sands spotted an open portal in the bulkhead. "Not likely," he said. He poked his head in the portal to have a look. It was the Warden's escape pod, outfitted and ready to launch. "Very nice. Our friend Oleg must have come across this when he was going through the ship's schematics." He motioned Ahmer over to have a look.

"What is it?"

"A way out." He gave Ahmer a significant look. "Room enough for two."

Now it was Ahmer's turn to back away from Sands. "We still have time to disarm the bomb."

Sands smiled crookedly. He had half a mind to grab the kid by the ears, toss him in the pod, and pile in after him. It was the smart play. He could save two lives, at least.

But Ahmer moved quickly away and turned to the pallets of C-4. "Seven minutes," he said, pointing out the readout on the timer.

Sands sighed and joined him. The timer looked simple enough, but the wiring seemed more complicated than necessary. Maybe it was a bluff to discourage meddlers, but maybe not. He tried tracing the wires, but quickly realized it was going to come down to an educated guess which one to cut.

"You have experience with such devices?"

"Not enough. I don't know if I can disarm it, but Angel was right." Sands tapped a module with a small antenna. "That's a radio receiver. A fail-safe. If we can find the transmitter, we can shut this thing off."

"Einstein?"

Sands nodded at Oleg's lifeless body. "I'd say he's nearby. You stay here. Get Catfish on the line. I'll—"

Sands was warned by the sudden look of terror in Ahmer's eyes, but it was too late.

Lunging out of the darkness with a multi-throated roar, Cerberus bowled them over, one mastiff head clamping its teeth on Ahmer's thigh and dragging him across the deck. Ahmer screamed as Sands leapt at the beast. Sands got a grip on the other mastiff's throat as the Chihuahua bit viciously at his arm and hands. Teeth like needles sank into one hand, causing Sand's to lose his grip. The mastiff bit down on his forearm with the force of a machine press. Sands gouged an eye with his free hand, but the beast held on. He ripped his other arm away from the gnawing Chihuahua, losing a wedge of flesh as he reached for his handgun. He shoved it under the mastiff's jaw and blew off the top of its head. It was a close call—he'd fired so close to his own arm he felt the burn of the muzzle blast. Batting the wildly snapping Chihuahua away, he emptied the clip into the beast's torso, and it went limp.

Sands pulled Ahmer away and inspected his wounds. The leg was badly mangled, but Sands thought it could be saved if they got help. He pulled off his shirt and ripped several strips from it to bind the wound.

Ahmer hadn't made a sound, but his labored breathing rasped in Sands' ears. His eyes were threatening to roll up into his head, but Sands shook him until he came back.

"Ahmer! Ahmer, stay with me, buddy!"

Ahmer's head lolled forward, but he was conscious. "The blood," he gasped. "It's bad."

"It didn't get the artery. You aren't going to bleed to death, okay? Help's on the way. I'm going after Einstein."

"Don't leave me here—with that." He eyed Cerberus' lifeless form.

"It's okay, Ahmer. It's dead."

Just to make Sands a liar, one mastiff head emitted a liquid growl. Sands slammed another clip in his pistol and shot it between the eyes.

"Okay, now it's dead."

The Chihuahua yapped.

Gritting his teeth, Sands fired again. There was a yip, and then nothing. He shoved the gun into Ahmer's hand. "If that thing sprouts another head, you empty the clip, okay?"

Ahmer smiled and passed out. Sands tapped his communicator. "Catfish! Catfish, come in!"

His receiver crackled. "Catfish here!"

In the background, Sands could hear gunshots. "Catfish, where are you? We got about five minutes to find Einstein if we're going to kill that bomb."

"I'm comin', Brother, but we're gettin' heavy resistance..."

There was more, but it was lost in the growl of static and gunfire.

"Catfish! Catfish!"

A heavy blow fell across Sands' back, crushing him to the deck. He went numb all over, as if his spine were broken. He kicked his legs weakly and rolled over onto his back. Standing over him was Einstein, one end of a splintered wooden spar in his hand.

"You shot my dog."

Sands stared up at him. Standing seven feet tall, lanky but hard-muscled, his hair standing up like it was permanently electrified, Einstein cut as frightening a figure as any Psych Sands had ever battled in the Arena. But the look in his eyes set him apart—somehow completely insane, but with an intelligence that was fully in control.

Einstein lunged without warning, driving the broken spar like a spear toward Sands' chest. Sands managed to roll out of the way, kicking Einstein's legs from under him.

Sands pushed himself to one knee, knife at the ready, but Einstein had already regained his feet. Swinging the spar like a club, he smashed Sands' hand, sending the knife to the deck. He swung again—wildly—and again, but Sands avoided each blow. Timing the swings, he lunged underneath, tackling Einstein around the ankles and sending the spar sailing against the bulkhead. They grappled on the deck, kicking, punching, and gouging, but Sands realized that if it came to a wrestling match, he might lose. Einstein wasn't quick, but he was incredibly strong.

Sands managed to push himself free and regain his feet. Still on one knee, Einstein struck an anvil-like blow to Sands' gut. They exchanged blows, but for every hay-maker Einstein landed, Sands landed three. Sidestepping a roundhouse swing that could have decapitated him, Sands slipped behind and put Einstein in a chokehold. If he could just hold on it would be over, but Einstein was so tall it was hard to get leverage.

Einstein flailed his arms, throwing Sands around like a cowboy riding a bull. But the flailing suddenly stopped, and Sands felt himself lifted off his feet as Einstein bent forward. Sands thought he was trying to throw him. He locked his legs around Einstein's torso, but a piercing pain turned his muscles to jelly. Einstein hadn't been trying to throw him. He had bent to pick up the spar and driven it through Sands' thigh.

Sands screamed, but somehow he held on, riding Einstein down to the deck. With a will to survive honed by three years in the Arena, he smashed Einstein's face into the deck. A lightning bolt of pain shot through Sands' body as the spar was jarred by the impact of their fall. A black pit seemed to open up before him. His arms and legs were four dead weights. But just as he was about to plunge into the void of unconsciousness something pulled him back. He heard a voice. "Go, Sands," it whispered in his ear. He saw a swirl of lights and faces. He saw Big Money. They all took up the chant: "Go, Sands, go!" He wondered how he had gotten back into the Arena, but the chant buoyed him up, sent the strength coursing back into his limbs. Einstein twisted beneath him, growling like an an-imal, but Sands held on. He crushed the madman's head into the riveted steel, again and again, until his face was a bloody mess.

Sands rolled off of Einstein onto his side. Almost blind with agony, he pounded the deck with his fist. No time to pass out, no time to die. The timer on the bomb read thirty-five seconds.

He dragged himself across the deck to the pallet of C-4. He got his good leg underneath and pulled himself up with his hands. Twenty-three seconds. He ripped open a pocket and pulled out his wire-cutters. Blinking sweat and blood from his eyes, he tried to trace the crucial wire.

Eighteen seconds. Twelve.

He shook his head, trying to clear the fog that was overtaking him. This wire. No, this one.

Five seconds.

No more time to think. This wire. He cut it.

Two seconds.

One.

Zero.

Sand squeezed his eyes shut, saying the fastest prayer he knew.

Nothing.

Sands opened his eyes. The timer was blinking zero, but there was no explosion, not even a pop or a fizzle.

"Oops."

The sweat rolling down Sands' back turned to ice. He pivoted on his one working leg to find Einstein, his face bloodied, his teeth broken, leering back at him as he braced himself against the open portal to the escape pod. In his hand was the transmitter.

"Sorry, Sands, but I don't believe in taking one for the team. This ship isn't going down until I'm safely off it."

Sands had lost his rifle, but he had another pistol on his hip. In an instant, he had it unholstered and aimed at Einstein's belly.

"Careful now." Einstein held the transmitter high. "One twitch of my thumb and we all go sky high."

Sands quickly swiped the sweat out of his eyes. He needed two hands to hold the gun steady.

"I'm listening."

"Good. You're a clear thinker. You can thank my special blend of Process for that. Pure nutrition. No additives."

Sands stared at him. Thoughts buzzed in his head like bees.

"That's right," Einstein said. "Formulated just for you."

Sands blinked his eyes hard—against the pain, against the weakness sweeping through his body, but especially against the buzzing in his head. He looked at this grotesque caricature of a man and he knew he was gazing into the eyes of his own personal tormentor.

"Why?"

"Because you're a killer, Sands. The best military training can produce. I wanted you at your peak when you went up against my laboratory creations. You see, controlling the mind by numbing it is easy. But you can't fight a war with the addicts on Limbo Deck."

"So that's what *Inferno* is all about. You're building your own zombie army."

"Not zombies. Controlled killers. These criminals owe a debt to society. This is my way of helping them pay it back."

"Okay," Sands said. "You've done the Bond villain bit. Now what?"

Einstein held his hands up in a surrendering pose, but with one thumb threatening the detonator button.

"Now you let me go. I get in the pod, I don't blow up the ship, and we all live to fight another day."

"Uh-huh. Once you're in the pod, what's to stop you reneging on the deal?"

Einstein shrugged. "That C-4 is going to make a big bang. Maybe by the time the pod is far enough away to be safe, I'll be out of range..."

Sands wasn't buying it.

"Or maybe," Einstein sneered. "You just have no choice."

Sands raised his gun higher, taking aim at Einstein's Adam's apple.

"Or maybe," Sands said, "I put a bullet through your spinal cord, and your trigger hand's dead before your brain even knows it."

Einstein blanched and stared wordlessly into the black void of the gun barrel. But Sands' strength was going fast, and his aim wavered.

Einstein smiled, showing red, jagged teeth.

"I don't think so, Sands. You can't make the shot. You can barely stand."

Blood trickled into Sands' eyes. He blinked it away, gritting his teeth as he strained to keep the bead of his pistol sight aligned with the finger's breadth target at the back of Einstein's neck. But the bead just kept vibrating, and the harder Sands strained the wilder it got.

He dropped the gun to the floor.

"A wise decision—"

And in one smooth motion, Sands swept his shotgun down from his shoulder holster and blasted Einstein's upheld trigger hand into a red spray.

Einstein screamed, clutching his hand as he collapsed backward into the portal.

Sands exhaled from deep in his chest and leaned back against the stack of C-4. He watched the shuddering, yowling figure of Einstein with satisfaction, imaging the cheers of sixty thousand *Inferno* prisoners if they could see how their enemy was finally crushed.

But Einstein's howls stopped. He shuddered again, but not with pain.

He was laughing.

Sands cringed from the sound. It was like nothing he had heard before, even from the Psychs in the Arena. Einstein was staring at the stump of his hand and laughing as if it was the funniest thing he had ever seen.

Rising up on his knees, Einstein lifted his stump. He held it defiantly before Sands' eyes. All the fingers had been blown away except one. The middle one.

The buzzing in Sands' head became a siren's wail. He stared at the macabre sight of Einstein, grinning and laughing madly at his upraised stump. In a frozen moment, Sands was unable to move, even to squeeze the trigger again on his shotgun, and Einstein punched a button with his elbow. The portal slammed shut and the pod ejected, Einstein's leering face receding to a point that lingered like a fierce light on the retina of Sands' eyes.

Sands heard a hatch bang open and boots scuff against the deck. Catfish was there, taking him by the shoulders and shouting his name. But Sands was as gone as Einstein, his consciousness a sinking pebble in the dark Arctic waters.

-22-

Yesterday is a cancelled check; tomorrow is a promissory note; today is the only cash you have—so spend it wisely.

—Kay Lyons

After four hours of waiting, Carrie was at last sitting on one of the mismatched chairs before the desk of the Justice International counsel she had seen just a week before. Emanuel was kneeling on the floor, hunched over a coloring book he had splayed out on the seat of the chair next to her. She had told him three times the floor was filthy and to sit in the chair properly and color in his lap, but she didn't have the energy to make it stick. It seemed she hadn't slept a minute since the bomb blast in Georgetown. Rick was at home, ill, and it worried her that he had not answered the phone in over an hour. She felt he should be in the hospital, but he wouldn't hear of it. The last time she got through he was annoyed because she had interrupted his sleep—for the second time that morning—so she hoped he was just asleep again, maybe with his phone muted.

She was feeling annoyed herself—exasperated by the long wait, despite the fact she had called ahead to make her "appointment." But there was no use complaining to people who took complaints for a living. Anyway, they would only point out it was her own doing. She had insisted on seeing the same counsel—Rappaport was the name on the card he had given her—despite the fact the secretary had told her she would be served faster if she took the first person available.

So now she was in Rappaport's cluttered cubicle, and she had to sit and wait another five—going on ten—minutes while he searched and rummaged and pulled at his chin, shuffling files and poring over papers with no more than an occasional grunt by way of communication. Finally, he looked up from the file he had spread out over his desk.

"You were in here just a week ago."

"That's right."

"Well, you were smart to ask for me, personally. I know they tell you to take first available counsel, but you don't want to have to bring a new person up to speed every time you walk in. Where's Major Guidry?"

Carrie swallowed before answering. "Ill."

Rappaport read her expression and went a little gray. "Oh. I'm very sorry to hear that. He was...?"

"He was on the Key Bridge when the bomb hit. Just turning onto it, actually. He was trapped there for over an hour."

"I understand people had to abandon their cars and escape on foot."

She looked down at her hands. They were clenched, her knuckles white. "That's right."

"May I ask what his prognosis is?"

She looked up quickly. "I'm surprised this place is open. So close to the blast site."

Rappaport took the hint not to press the question. "We're upwind. The fallout zone is just a mile east. But we've had the place swept three times. We'll do it again every few days, just to be sure. We're safe here."

Emanuel, sensing the tension in his mother's voice, put aside his coloring and lay his head in her lap. She brushed her fingers through his hair. It was the same ashy brown as Sands'.

"Well," Rappaport said. "Did someone from our office contact you?"

"I came in on my own."

"I see. But it's only been a week—"

"You said that already."

Rappaport smiled. "So I did. Sorry. I think I know why you're here."

"I have to know if Sands was on that ship."

Rappaport cleared his throat. "That information hasn't been made public."

"But you have it. Don't you?"

"Ms. Guidry, the information we handle is often very sensitive. We can't—"

"If you know, you have to tell me. I'm not leaving until you do."

Rappaport's head bobbed once, halfway between a nod and a bow. "Excuse me."

He smoothly negotiated the maze of boxes and files that filled his cubicle and exited behind her. Carrie turned to watch the top of his head bob above the partitions and round the corner to the cubicle of his neighbor. She heard hushed voices that talked over one another with increasing vehemence—until they abruptly stopped. Rappaport returned momentarily with a slip of paper in his hand and said, "I'll make a call."

He sat at his desk, opened a drawer, and pulled out a cheap phone that Carrie recognized from watching too many crime dramas as a "burner." He placed a battery in the phone, powered it up, and dialed the number on the slip of paper. He dropped the slip into a shredder. In a moment, he said "Rappaport," and then a phrase of nonsense that sounded like a code. "I need you to check a name on the *Perdido* manifest. That's right. Last name Simon, first name Sands." He glanced at Carrie. "No, you heard correctly. Last name Simon."

The JI counsel took on that expression one does when put on hold. He tried to be casual as he flipped through the papers in Sands' file, but it was obvious he felt Carrie's eyes burning into him. When it appeared the other person had come back on the line, he turned in his chair so that she was left looking at his back.

"Yes?" His voice was quiet, like one who expects to deliver bad news. "That's right. First name Sands."

Carrie's heart sank into her stomach. There was something final in the way he had repeated those words.

"You're sure? Okay, thank you."

He half-turned in his chair, still not facing her. He broke down the phone and returned it and the battery to his desk. Carrie watched him, wanting to scream at him to tell her what he had learned, but she felt she couldn't breathe.

He put his elbows on the desktop, hands clasped before him, and made a poor attempt at a smile. "Ms. Guidry, I want you to understand one thing before I tell you this."

"Oh, no—no, no—"

Rappaport held up his hands. "Please. It's not what you think. Hear me out. We have a partial manifest of a ship called *The Perdido*. We believe *The Perdido* is the illegal prison ship that was sunk in the Sea of Japan. The manifest is two years old. We know—or at least we have very good reason to believe—that anyone named on that manifest was in fact on *The Perdido* as of two years ago. What we don't know is who may have been on the ship prior to that and removed, or who may have been transported to the ship in the time since. We also do not know the names of any prisoners on any of the other five or six black rafts we believe are in existence."

"Please," Carrie groaned, in physical pain. "Can you just tell me?"

"I'm sorry, I'm not trying to be cruel, but don't read more into this than there is. The name Sands Simon does not appear on that list."

Carrie sobbed with relief and clasped Emanuel in a smothering embrace.

"As I say. It's not necessarily good news, but it definitely isn't bad news."

-23-

"The time has come," the Walrus said, "To talk of many things; Of shoes—and ships—and sealing wax. Of cabbages and Kings—And why the sea is boiling hot—And whether pigs have wings."

—Lewis Carroll

Sands awoke from what he thought was a nightmare—but no, there it was, right before his eyes on the video monitor that hung from the ceiling beyond the foot of his bed: Dr. Henry Brzinski, staring down at him from behind a desk in some nondescript, bunker-like redoubt, a bloody Bible at his elbow, the twin flags of the United States of America and the New Freedom Party behind him, one angled over each shoulder. His expression was grave, but from years of close observation of the Doctor's moods Sands recognized the spark of fevered excitement in his eyes.

"My fellow Americans, my fellow citizens of the world. I come to you today with a heavy heart, but an unbowed spirit...."

Sands felt fuzzy-headed, disoriented—but as he took in his surroundings he realized he had seen this room before, sometime earlier in the morning, or perhaps the previous day. There had been a doctor and a nurse, and faces familiar and strange crowding around him. He thought he must be in some kind of infirmary, but where? Had *The Inferno* survived? Was he still aboard the ship? He tried to think, but Brzinski's voice nagged for his attention.

"It is my sad duty to report that President William Stockdale is dead, gunned down by a North Korean agent who had infiltrated the innermost circles of the White House. The assassin, Secretary of State Ken Lum, is also dead. I take no joy in telling you that I have just taken the oath of office as President Stockdale's successor."

So it was a nightmare, but a real one. Sands realized that the monitor over his bed was not like the ones he was accustomed to on *Inferno*. It looked more like a regular TV set. And it had a bright red power button.

He grabbed a box of tissues from his bedside table. He hurled it at the power button bullseye, but it bounced away without effect.

"The chain reaction of nuclear strikes initiated by the terrorists Kim Jong-Seung and Radwan Karga have created great carnage—including devastation to our own precious capital—but I want to assure you that global nuclear war has been averted."

Sands hurled a plastic cup, but it was even less effective than the box of tissues. He cursed under his breath as Brzinski droned on.

"Karga and Kim have been eliminated, their nuclear arsenals destroyed. Pyongyang and the whole of North Korea have been reduced to radioactive rubble, never to trouble the peace-loving peoples of the world again."

Sands spotted two shoes at the side of his bed—perfect missiles. He rolled over as far as he could and retrieved them. Taking careful aim, he launched the first. It made a satisfying *thwack!* as it struck the monitor, but it only succeeded in making Brzinski go a little green.

"Hey!" Sands shouted. "Nurse! Somebody!"

He threw his other shoe. It hit Brzinski squarely in the nose, but he just nattered on.

"Total, unimaginable disaster has been averted, but the threat remains. That is why as of noon today, I have declared martial law..."

"Hey! Somebody turn this shit off!"

Sands sat up and tried to swing his legs over the side of the bed. They didn't make it. It took several tries, with a lot of help from his arms, to get his feet on the floor. He felt a stabbing pain shoot up and down his entire left side, but if he had to crawl, Sands was determined to shut up Brzinski. Fortunately, Ahmer entered before he could topple himself completely out of bed.

"Sands! You're awake!"

"Ahmer, will you please turned that damned thing off!"

"Of course! Yes!"

It was only then that Sands noticed that Ahmer was on crutches, one leg bandaged from ankle to crotch. He hobbled gamely over to the monitor and shut it off.

"Thanks."

Ahmer hobbled over to Sands' bedside and helped get his legs back up in a comfortable position.

"How long have I been out?"

"Five days."

"Five days!"

"You were awake yesterday for while, but not very long. Bad infection. Sepsis from your wound. Dr. Abdallah says we almost lost you."

"Who's Dr. Abdallah?"

"Your friend. Rashid."

"Well, I'll be damned. I thought that doctor bit was just a line to get out of his cage."

"Oh, no. Dr. Abdallah is very top physician."

Ahmer pressed the comm button by Sands' bed. "He's awake." To Sands he said, "The others will be glad to see you looking so well."

"So I guess the ship didn't blow up."

"Indeed not."

"Prop me up, will you?"

Ahmer found the bed control and raised Sands' head until he was comfortable.

"Thanks."

Catfish and Victoria appeared at the door.

"Hey," Catfish called, "are you ready to get off your sorry ass and start kickin' some!"

Sands put his hands behind his head and leaned back on his pillow.

"Not me. I've earned a vacation."

Victoria approached his bed. He took her in like a cool drink.

"Hey, Sands."

"Hey Victoria. Looks like we made it, huh?"

They squeezed hands.

"I wouldn't get too comfortable," Catfish interrupted. "You need to hear what's going on."

"We're alive. What else matters?"

"We're alive, but for how long?" Victoria said. "As soon as the Six Hundred figure out what happened they'll come after us."

Sands didn't appreciate being slapped with such a big dose of reality so soon after being rousted from slumber. It was the military all over again. He looked at Catfish. "How much time you figure we got?"

"Hard to say. We knocked out the transponders on all five ships, so they won't be able to track us that way."

"*Five* ships?"

"All the surviving black rafts," Victoria said. "They're all here."

"It's a regular flotilla," Catfish said.

Sands whistled. "So as far as the Six Hundred knows, their plan to sink the ships was successful."

"We hope so."

"Well, it was good thinking anyway."

"Don't tell me. It was Ahmer that thought of it."

Sands looked at Ahmer, who was trying not to beam too proudly. Sands gave him his best fatherly nod.

"But even if they can't track us," Catfish continued, "we need supplies. We've got about three hundred thousand hungry convicts on five ships—and now that they've gotten off Process, ain't none of 'em too keen to get back on it."

"So what needs to be done?"

"You tell us."

Sands immediately got the implication. "You're barkin' up the wrong tree, Brother."

"Are we?" Victoria fixed a fierce gaze on him that affected him like no other. "The only thing keeping these people in line right now is fresh food and the hope that their hero—The Sandman—is still alive to lead them."

Sands was about to reply, when Rashid pushed open the door. Bao, Desmond, and Lani stampeded in after him.

"It's true!" Desmond exclaimed.

Lani shouted Sands' name and practically leaped into his arms. The bear hug she inflicted on him sent knives of pain through his cracked ribs.

"Okay, okay," Sands said, his voice between a grunt and a plea.

Coming to herself, Lani quickly backed away. "I'm glad to see you're feeling better," she said demurely.

"We all are," Bao seconded.

Sands gave them a wincing smile.

Rashid pressed Sands on the shoulder, grinning down on him like a pleased midwife.

Sands patted his hand. "Thanks, Doc."

From outside there was a rumble, the sound of thousands gathering and voicing their excitement.

"Sounds like the word is out," Catfish observed.

"I'm no leader," Sands protested.

They all looked at him, their expressions saying otherwise.

"C'mon, man, I just came out of a coma!"

"Yesterday you came out of a coma," Rashid corrected. "Today you've only been—" He turned to Catfish. "What is the military term?"

"Goldbricking."

"Yes. Goldbricking."

"Thanks, Doc. Call it what you want, but I need to get my strength up. I don't know if I can even stand."

"Bullshit," Catfish countered.

"But—"

"They just want to see you, Sands," Victoria said gently. "You don't have to say anything."

Sands turned to Ahmer, but there was no help there.

"They're waiting for you, Sands."

Ahmer offered Sands one of his crutches. What could he do but take it?

Sands swung his legs over the side of the bed. He felt a twinge of pain, but his limbs cooperated as they hadn't before. He pulled himself up on one crutch, Ahmer slipping an arm around his side. Sands draped one trunk-like arm over the young man's narrow shoulders, and together they took their first awkward steps toward the hatch.

Moments later, they emerged from the Command Deck, like twins, clutching each other and their crutches as they made their way out onto the gangway of the Bridge. Catfish and the others followed closely, ready to bear them up if they stumbled, but trying not to be too obvious.

The Top-deck was flooded with *Inferno* inmates— thousands of them, with thousands more undoubtedly watching on the monitors below decks. Sands saw in the distance the same scene reflected on the decks of the other black rafts, all lined up within a few hundred yards of one another.

As Sands became visible over the rail a massive cheer went up. It echoed across the waters, from one ship to another, and the inmates began chanting his name, just as they had done so many times when he appeared in the Arena.

Overwhelmed, Sands hung back, but Ahmer and his other friends pressed him forward with silent encouragement.

"All you have to do is wave," Victoria said in his ear, but Sands noticed that a microphone had been set up at the rail. Waving wouldn't be enough, he thought. They wanted to hear something.

He stepped to the rail and took the microphone.

Another cheer went up, greater than the first, hitting Sands like a warm updraft that buoyed him up. He raised his hands for silence—a gesture he had never seen elicit among the raucous *Inferno* inmates anything less than louder choruses of jeers—but silence they gave him.

In a long, still moment, he could hear nothing but the lapping of waves against *Inferno's* hull and the keening of seabirds.

"I, uh—"

There was no amplification. Bao stepped up and adjusted the mic. Sands tried it again.

"I'm not much on giving speeches." It wasn't a rhetorical ploy. Sands really had no idea what to say.

"That's okay," a voice down front shouted. "Dregs ain't much for listenin' to 'em!"

Laughter from those within earshot. Ripples as others repeated the quip. Sands smiled with them, holding up one hand in acknowledgment.

"That's right," he said, his voice suddenly full. "They call us Dregs." He clapped Ahmer on the shoulder. "They call us Drones. We're the expendables. The disappeared. The throw-away people. That's how the world thinks of us. But when I look out at you, you know what I see?"

He paused. The whole ship seemed to lean in to catch his next words.

"I see an army."

He didn't know where the thought came from, but the instant the cheers began, he knew he had chosen the right words.

"They tried to lock us away. They tried to control us. They tried to kill us. They tried to forget us. Why? Because they're afraid of us. They're afraid of power in the hands of the people. And you know what I say to that? *They'd better be!*"

The cheers were reinforced by the stamping of feet. The whole ship trembled.

"That's right." Sands was feeding off their energy now. His reluctance was forgotten. His pain was forgotten. "They tried to forget us. But I'm telling you right now—*we won't be forgotten!*"

Sands pounded the rail with his fist. "They want a fight? I say let's bring it! I say let's take it to them before they take it to us! Let's hit 'em before they *know* what's hit 'em! They like to play battle? Let's give 'em *WAR!*"

The thousands erupted. Sands pumped his fist in the air, punctuating each thrust with the shout of "War! War!" until they took up the chant.

He nodded with satisfaction. It was all he had, but maybe it was enough. Letting his crutch fall away, he turned and marched, with all the poise and dignity he could summon, back onto the Bridge.

The instant he was out of sight, he slumped. Catfish caught him, bearing up his full weight until Desmond could push the Captain's chair forward and help ease him into it.

"I'm all right," Sands said. "Just need to catch my breath."

Bao brought him some water. Sands took it and gulped it down.

"Thanks."

Rashid bent down to check his bandages, to make sure they were still in place. Lani brought him a damp towel, applying it to his forehead and the back of his neck. They all buzzed and fretted over him like so many nursemaids—all but Victoria.

Hands on hips, she said, "Nice speech. What now?"

"We head north."

"North?"

"You know," Catfish said, "we're almost at the Pole already. We keep headin' north we're gonna wind up goin' south."

"That's right. To the scene of the crime." Sands was exhausted. The chair held him so fast, so comfortingly, he wondered when he would ever be able to get up out of it again. But his mind was clear. Out on the deck, when his mouth had managed to talk faster than his brain could think, something snapped within him. He felt like he knew just what to do.

"What scene of what crime?" Catfish asked.

"The one place nobody will think to look for us." He waited until they all finished looking questions at each other.

"Korea."

"Korea?" Catfish echoed. "As in *South* Korea?"

"*North* Korea."

"Ain't you heard, man? The whole peninsula's been nuked. I'm talkin' burnin' rocks and boilin' seas. Sodom and Gomorrah-style Biblical destruction."

"I know."

"You *know?*"

"Well, I seen it on the tee-vee, so it must be true."

The others all looked at one another as if they thought Sands had lost it. It came down to Ahmer to speak up for him.

"Sands is right. They said Seoul and Pyongyang were hit. That's two cities. Not whole peninsula."

"But the President—" Lani began.

"Don't call him that."

Sands regretted his sharp tone, but it made him smile to see how quickly Ahmer was there to give Lani's shoulder a consoling squeeze.

"Well, one thing is certain." Everyone was surprised to hear from Rashid. "No one with any sense will be going there. Sometimes, the hunted can only survive by going where the hunter fears to follow."

Shrugs and nods of reluctant assent went up all around.

"The way I see it," Sands said, "if Hell is all they've left us...We'll take it."

Catfish was out of arguments. He turned to Bao and Desmond. "You heard the Commander. Turn her north. Set a course for Korea."

He looked at Sands and shook his head. "I'll pass the word to the other ships' captains. I don't know how I'm gonna explain it."

"Just give 'em the course, for now. If you want, you can tell 'em we're using what's left of the ice caps to discourage others from following. Leave off the part about Korea. Tomorrow, or maybe the next day, after I've gotten my strength up, we'll call a meeting and I'll put it out there myself."

"Okay, Sands."

He saluted. Surprised, Sands skipped a beat before he saluted back. Catfish turned and headed for the comm.

It took an hour to get the five massive ships up to full power and turned in the direction of their new course. They lined up, with *Inferno* taking the lead, in a tight vee formation, six football fields between ships, two miles from nearest to farthest. With their sterns turned against a golden sun that rested low on the horizon, the ships' five shadows stretched long before them, like the strides of giants across the waters.

THE END

For background, graphics, and new developments in the
Inferno 2033 universe, visit our website at
www.inferno-2033.com

For more exciting fiction by these authors
and others, visit The Journey Press at
www.thejourneypress.com

www.ingramcontent.com/pod-product-compliance
Lightning Source LLC
Chambersburg PA
CBHW031245120726
47905CB00002B/726